Tattered Hearts

KC ENDERS

ISBN-13: 979-8-9911880-1-2

Tattered Hearts

To my husband.
And to my family—those of love and those of blood.

LETTER TO THE READER

Dearest Reader,

Have you ever had a dream so big, it's seemingly out of reach? One that, when it actually happens, you're not quite sure whether to laugh, cry or pinch yourself? That's what this whole writing thing is for me. A dream come true.

This book was previously published as part of a world established by another author through her own amazing and heartfelt stories. I will forever be grateful for the opportunity to be a part of that. The timing was perfect since I had a character from my series of standalones who was speaking to me. Chloe Triplett needed a chance at salvation. Her story was introduced in Tombstones, *the final installment of my* Beekman Hills *series —maybe. Who knows, there could always be another one!*

So, if you've read Broken, you've already read this story. A handful of names have been changed, some minor self-edits made, but the gist of the story is the same.

Beekman Hills is my hometown, it's where I grew up. Where I fell in love and experienced heartbreak, because, let's be honest, you can't have one without the other... or so they say. But my characters have a habit of jumping books, sharing space, and showing up wherever they want. So, when you're done here, go check them out! Pour yourself a beverage and dive into the Irish pub in small town New York. Listen to sweet nothings whispered in Gaelic. Find out what's so special about the lead guitarist in the band. And don't forget about going back to where it all started for Chloe Triplett...

All my love,

KC

PROLOGUE

Chloe

A hush falls over the cemetery as the doors of the hearse creak open.

My husband's best friend, Jack, walks with me behind Dallas's casket, quietly supporting me. I reach out, searching for one last moment with my dead husband. I'm not ready to let him go. I'll never be ready to let him go.

Jack escorts me to the chairs set in two precise rows, occupied by my son, my parents, and my brothers. Dallas's parents, his sister. Even Dallas's granddad—God bless him—is here, refusing a seat, instead leaning on his cane.

"Thank you," I whisper as Jack lowers himself into the chair next to me.

The chaplain speaks, his voice ringing out sad and clear, but nothing he says registers. How can it? My husband is dead, lying in the flag-draped box in front of me. It's too soon. We had too many things left undone in our lives for him to be ripped away from us now.

How am I going to do this on my own?

The air changes as the uniformed service members shift, standing at attention, tall and proud. Jesse Dennison, the team sergeant for Dallas's unit, moves into position next to the casket. Even though I know what's coming, I flinch as he starts the final roll call.

"Staff Sergeant Riojas," he calls in a booming voice.

"Here, Team Sergeant," comes the response.

"Sergeant First Class Baker."

"Here, Team Sergeant."

The crack in my chest deepens.

"Sergeant Vance."

"Here, Team Sergeant."

"Sergeant Triplett."

Silence. And my heart stalls in my chest.

"Sergeant Dallas Triplett."

Crippling pain sears through me, ripping me apart.

"Sergeant Dallas H. Triplett."

My life is in tatters, my love lying broken at my feet.

The only sound is my gasped sob. Jack wraps an arm around me, pulling me back from the brink. Back from where I reach out for Dallas, my hand grasping at nothing but air. I'm only vaguely aware that Jack is supporting me, holding me up. Holding me back because, without him, I think I could throw myself across Dallas's casket.

I don't know how much more I can take.

I don't know how I can live without him.

The crisp report of rifle fire echoes across the hill.

Once.

Twice.

Three times.

Jake startles next to me, crying out, "My daddy. I want my daddy."

Tears stream down my face, unbidden and unwelcome.

The chilling strains of "Taps" rise up. Sunlight glints off the bugle as the flag is removed from Dallas's casket, precisely folded, and carefully smoothed. Three brass shell casings rest on top.

With my husband's flag clutched tightly to my chest and Jake sobbing as Jack tends to us, I say my final good-bye to the only man I've ever loved.

ONE

Chloe

five years later

Deep breath in, slowly exhale. Deep breath in, slowly exhale.

Anxiety pulls at every cell in my body, panic looming, staring me down. My gaze darts around the inside of the gas station as I try to commit each face to memory, looking for a sign that one of them is harboring a secret. Searching for a tell, a flash of metal, a nervous twitch that comes just before the strike.

"Mom, can I get a soda?" Jake asks.

I scan the faces again, and with a terse nod, my hand clamped firmly on his shoulder, I guide my son to the wall lined with cups and fountain drinks.

"You're doing it again, jeez. I can get it," he whines, shrugging against my hand.

I miss my sweet, polite, respectful little boy and wonder for a hot minute who replaced him with this prepubescent Jekyll. Or is it Hyde? It doesn't really matter at the moment because we just need to get out of here—and fast.

"Quickly, please," I tell him, paying more attention to the bodies filtering in and out of the store than I am to Jake.

Concerned about what is taking so long, I dart a glance to Jake, only to see it's not just a soda he's getting. The biggest cup they have is nearly overflowing with the sugariest, most caffeinated bright red beverage available.

"Jacob Wyatt Triplett, what are you thinking?" I scold.

He, of course, rolls his eyes and gives me a frustrated sigh that would test the patience of Mother Teresa. There are only so many things I can concentrate on at once, and right now, I need to focus on our safety.

"Put a lid on it, and let's go," I say through gritted teeth.

I steer him to the register, already holding my debit card and hating that I have my back to the room. I feel exposed. Vulnerable. Scared.

Jake stands next to me, the ridiculous vat of soda clutched possessively in both of his hands. And with each step we take toward the register, he takes a half-step to the side, putting distance between us.

I swallow, trying to push down the lump that's formed in my throat.

"That's three dollars and twenty-two cents," the cashier says, sounding tinny and far away, already ringing up the next customer on the register to her left.

I shove my card into the slot, and the sun glints off something shiny, reflecting a burst of light into my eyes. I flinch, reaching blindly for Jake but he's not there. He's just out of reach, at the end of the counter, looking at brightly colored candies, oblivious to the world.

With a metallic flash, panic surges through me in a way it hasn't in a very long time. I bend my knees, lowering into a crouch, and step toward Jake. As my fingers brush against the sandy-brown hair curling behind his ear, what sounds like a gunshot slices through my heart, and the feel of shrapnel bites through the backs of my legs.

My only thought is of getting to my son, keeping him safe.

Another flash, and a hand latches on to my shoulder, pulling me back, away from Jake. Away from the object of my singular focus.

My heart thrashes in my chest, my blood like lead in my veins.

My lungs contract, pulling in tiny bursts of air, but I can't breathe. There's no in and out right now. Just in.

My eyes are wide, but I see nothing as black dots fill my vision, tunneling and then finally closing in on me.

I'm dying.

My eleven-year-old son is going to be all alone. How long will it take his uncle Jack to find him? At least he'll have a real family again. Jack will step into the dad role, and Kate will treat him like one of her own. Siblings. Jake will finally have the siblings he so desperately wanted before his dad died. He already fights with their twin boys like he is the older brother, and God knows he watches over their daughter, Hays, like it's his mission in life.

He'll be okay. He'll be okay. He has to be okay.

JAKE'S VOICE is the first to filter through my fuzzy head. Not so much the words, just the sound of him chatting—but to whom? I don't recognize the deep rumble asking Jake questions, but instead of pumping up my anxiety, the deep timbre soothes me.

Awareness slowly comes back to me in drips and pieces, and I take stock of myself. My head is killing me, and the tiles of the floor pressed to my back are cold.

The buzz and chattering of conversation between Jake and the stranger take form.

"Her name is Chloe Triplett. I'm Jake. We just moved here, so we don't really know anybody yet," Jake says.

A loud slurp through the straw tells me I've been out long enough for him to finish most of his drink.

Three warm fingers wrap around my arm and press into my wrist below the meat of my thumb. I don't know if it's actually possible, but I feel each heartbeat thrum against that pressure. And each thump seems to be stronger, more electrified than the last. Pushing harder, beating sturdier. Like my heart is grasping at something just out of reach. Something exciting but safe. Something new yet soothingly familiar at the same time.

My eyes flutter open, and I immediately seek out my son. When I find him safe, totally okay, breath whooshes from my lungs.

"Hey, buddy," I croak, my voice raspy and quiet.

What I get in return is a dramatic eye roll and a look of absolute disgust from my almost teenager.

"Why do you do that? Can we just go now?"

My thoughts jump from concern for my precious boy—the last link I have to his father—to the obnoxious reminder of why tigers have been known to eat their young. I push myself up to sitting and try to shake off the big hand still firmly wrapped around my arm.

"Slow down, ma'am." The deep voice only registers in my brain in that it's connected to the man holding me in place. Or maybe he's holding me up.

"Jake." The warning in my voice is clear to everyone standing, gawking, except my kid, if facial expressions are any indication.

I shove my feet underneath me and push myself up with my free hand, barely acknowledging that the stranger next to me is in fact helping me to stand. Panic bleeds through when I call to Jake again, and he turns and bolts out the door. I scoop my wristlet from the floor near my feet and search for my keys, but they're nowhere to be seen, and I can't let Jake be out there alone. I can't trust him to make good choices, even for an eleven-year-old. His shitty judgment, which gets him into trouble, is half the reason we're here in Virginia. The other half... I just can't go there right now.

With as much dignity as I can muster, I mumble, "Thank you," to the kind stranger next to me and hurry out of the convenience store.

I close my eyes and blow out a sigh of relief at the sight of my kid, pouty and sulking, standing with his back against the side of my car.

"Hey, you've got to stick with me, Jake. I know you were embarrassed, but you can't just take off like that. Especially now, in a new place, right?" I keep my voice low and calm because fear is a close friend of embarrassment, and neither party is particularly welcome at the moment.

My friend, Kate, refers to it as the teacher voice. As a kindergarten teacher, hers is way different from mine, though there are times that I think her students are more mature than the ones I deal with in high school.

"This is stupid," Jake mumbles. "What if somebody saw you? What if they recognize me in school on Monday? I'll literally die of... of..." He screws up his face as he searches for the right word.

"Mortification," I offer, leaning against the side of the car next to him, reveling in the bright winter sun. January in Virginia is a stark contrast from what New York would feel like now.

"Yeah, that," he says, focusing on the scuffed, frayed toes of his sneakers.

I reach over and take a quick sip from the last of his soda, handing it back before the scowl fully settles on his face.

"The good news is, anyone your age is in school right now, so they missed the entire thing. You're safe from humiliation for at least another couple of days." I manage to let only a half-smile find its way to my face.

"And the bad news?" he asks, pushing his hair out of his face.

I nod toward the store. "We have to go back in there together and find my keys. I dropped them when I went down."

His face scrunches up, and for a brief moment, I have a glimpse of sweet Jake. My little boy shows his face at the strangest times—when I least expect it and, if I'm lucky, when I need it the most.

TWO

Miles

I step up to the register and push a burrito and a liter bottle of water toward the center of the counter.

A second burrito, an energy drink, and a couple of tallboys appear next to my lunch. "Add this to his tab, too." Chance Robinson flashes his grin at me and then turns his attention to the cute blonde behind the counter.

The cashier looks to me for confirmation, and I give her a quick nod.

"Really, man?" I nudge one of the tall cans of beer he grabbed. "You prepping for happy hour already?" I ask, sticking my card into the reader. I should have gotten a bottle of ibuprofen and a sports drink to help with my hangover. I should seriously consider finding a better way to spend my evenings than drinking with my coworker.

He stretches his arms over his head before dragging one hand down his face. The sound of several days' growth of dark stubble rasps across his palm. "I'm like a Boy Scout, man. Ready for anything." A shit-eating grin slides across his face as he winks at the cashier.

She's all but drooling at his attention. *Poor girl.*

"Don't bother, sweetheart. This heartless bastard is called Tin Man for a reason," I tell her.

A set of keys skitters across the floor as I take a step back. I scoop them up and glance around. "Did that woman have her keys when she took off?"

"Who, Sleeping Beauty?" Chance asks, never taking his eyes off the chick behind the counter. "Go save the day, Clark. Get on that."

I snag my lunch and walk toward the glass door. She's leaning against the side of a dark red SUV, one of the small crossover ones. Her dark hair, piled high on her head, sways as she nods toward the store. Loose curls tease against the pale, creamy skin of her neck.

I push through the door and drop my aviators down over my eyes as I approach. "Ma'am, you dropped these," I say, stepping off the curb. A medallion jangles against the key fob as I hold the keys out for her.

The kid throws me some serious shade, but the gorgeous woman cringes when she looks over her shoulder, embarrassment tingeing her cheeks pink. Black hair, sparkling blue eyes—she looks more like Snow White than Sleeping Beauty.

Gingerly, she takes the keys from me and hits the unlock button three times in rapid succession. "Thank you for that, in there. For everything really. I'm, uh... That hasn't happened in a while. I'm... Well, just thank you." She waves a hand toward the store and then me. A tight, nervous smile pinches at the corner of her mouth.

"You okay to drive? Need me to call someone for you?" The offer automatically tumbles from my mouth. It's what I do. Swoop in, do a good deed, try to do even more.

"We don't know anybody here. I just told you that," the kid, Jake, says. Attitude dripping from every syllable.

"Jacob Wyatt Triplett, mind your manners and get in the car," she says. No nonsense.

She comes across as a take-no-shit mom. But when the car door flies open, a white-and-black dappled hound dog lumbers out, wandering toward the back of the car before he stops and stares at me. It's a little unnerving, the way he looks at me like he knows me.

"Damn it, Bronson. Get back here."

She lunges around the car door and snags the dog by the collar, guiding him back into the car. The dog grunts and settles into the seat, staring me down. She cuts a warning look at her son and closes the door. She rests a palm on her forehead. Shoulders slumped beneath her oversize cable-knit sweater.

Defeated. This beautiful woman looks absolutely defeated.

The last time I saw that look was the day my world turned upside down and the pieces of my life tumbled all around me. I shake my head, pushing the ghosts of the past away and focus on the woman in front of me.

"You sure you're okay?" I'm drawn to her. I want to press my fingers to the soft skin on the inside of her wrist again, feel the way her pulse sped up when she looked into my eyes.

"I am, and thank you." She smiles and slides the key ring back and forth through the single key and fob, the medallion glinting in the sunlight. "I'm so sorry you had a front row seat to the shitshow I'm hosting today." Another quick, "Thank you," and she steps past, barely brushing up against me as she climbs in the driver's seat.

With an awkward wave, she's nothing but receding taillights turning at the corner by the time Chance saunters out of the store.

He taps at his phone with one hand as a bag swings from the other. "Out of your league, Clark," Chance mumbles, using the stupid-ass nickname he gave me, as he glances up from his phone.

He thinks it's hysterical to fuck with my call sign. The rest of the former SEALs we work with stick with calling me Superman. As if that's not bad enough.

"Shut up, asshole." I climb into my pickup—my baby—and run my palm across the polished walnut steering wheel, cool in the winter chill.

Chance folds himself in and drops his head back, banging it on the glass behind the bench seat. "She's hot as fuck, man, but she's got a kid."

He's just knocking it out of the fucking park with his observations.

"Saw that. Thanks for pointing it out though." I rev the engine, hoping she doesn't die on me.

Nothing more than a little hiccup, a minor belch of exhaust, and she lurches forward out of the lot before settling nicely into second gear.

"Fucking hell, Miles," Chance bitches, wiping a hand down the front of his shirt. "You need to fix this piece of shit. See if Amarre can help you figure out what's up with it and lock that shit down. Or better yet, get some new fucking wheels. Something from this century."

"Crossing a line, man," I say out the side of my mouth. Nobody talks shit about my '52 Chevy pickup, Maggie.

I found her in a heap, just as down on her luck as I was. After dragging her home, I spent the better part of a year pouring all my pain and frustration into her. And in doing so, I brought her broken ass back from the brink. She did the same for me.

Chance isn't wrong though. I do need some insight on why my girl is stuttering all of a sudden, and I don't know anyone better with old cars than Blake Amarre. At the next stoplight, I tap out a quick text to see if he's in town, shoving my phone under my thigh when I'm done.

Still an active SEAL, Blake has stuck with the teams, but he's worked closely with Fire Born Security for years. Personally, I think it's just a matter of time before he joins us full-time.

The ride back to the office is mostly silent, punctuated only by the occasional grumbling complaint from Chance. He's got no room to complain about my truck when he jumps at the opportunity to ride along instead of driving himself.

Back inside, I set the bag of food on the corner of my desk and slide into my chair. I sift through a backlog of emails while I eat, making note of project changes and deadlines that have shifted. I love my work. Never saw myself in the private sector, but it was the right thing for me to do. Sometimes though, I need more. More to do. More tasks to fill my time. A family. Just... more.

Hours pass, and yet my mind continues to bounce right back to the fainting beauty from the convenience store. I don't know what her story is, but I know PTSD when I see it, and that woman has been through something. I roll my shoulders and force my head from side to side until a satisfying crack echoes through the room.

"Jesus, Clark. That can't be good for you," Erin Amarre, Blake's wife, mutters as she drops a stack of files on my desk.

Chance's personality is obviously infecting the office if Erin is calling me that now.

A laugh pushes its way out of my nose as I lean back in my chair and knead at the knot that's firmly twisting at the base of my skull. Maybe I should cut out early today. Grab a drink—or six. *So much for cutting back on drinking.*

"I need a breakdown on this situation in Africa. Doesn't have to be right this minute; end of the week is fine," Erin adds quickly.

I flip through the file on top. Relief settles in sweetly as I appreciate just how organized she is. "Fine?" I ask, lifting a brow at her word choice. Fine is never good. Nothing is *ever* fine.

"Legit fine. I have a sit-down with Jason on Monday and want the weekend to go through your evaluation," Erin says, referring to Jason Grant, one of the owners of the company. She shifts toward the door and moves to leave.

"Hey, Erin?" I call, stopping her before she leaves. "You think Blake would mind taking a look at Maggie for me? She's stuttering, and I can't put my finger on what the problem is. I texted him earlier, but he hasn't gotten back to me yet."

I hate asking for favors, for help. Any of that stuff. I'm the guy who steps in and fills the gap. The one everyone can depend on to take care of shit.

Laughter floats over her shoulder. "I'm sure he'd love to get his hands on her. What is it with you boys and naming your cars? He's been swamped at work, but come by the house for dinner next week. I'll let Blake know you need his delicate touch, and maybe you can remind Tyler that playing rugby is a privilege. He's tanking in math. *Shit.* I need to make an appointment with his new teacher." She pulls her phone from her pocket and taps at the screen. "Next week though. See if Chance'll come with you. He looks like he needs a home-cooked meal or an intervention—something."

Minutes later, she's out the door for the night, still tapping wildly at her phone.

I thumb through the files she left me, making notes. Erin might not need this immediately, but it's not like I have anything other than work and coaching two rugby teams to fill my time. No one waiting on me at home, just an empty apart-ment, a glass of whiskey, and whatever takeout I end up grab-bing on my way.

Almost an hour later, I shut down my computer and wind my way through the office.

"Thank fuck," Chance grumbles as I hit the last set of lights. "You finally taking off? Want to stop by Chick's, grab a drink? Maybe some ass?" He's sprawled back in the reception-ist's chair, a smattering of dust under where his boots are crossed on top of the desk.

"Aw, you waiting around for me, Tin Man?" I nod to the mess he's making and say, "You clean that up, and I'll meet you there."

Boots thud to the floor, and the chair screeches back until it hits the wall. Chance swipes a lazy hand across the surface of the desk, sending dust flying. "I'm good. I'll just ride with you," he says, following me out the door.

It's probably for the best anyway. If Chance rides with me, I won't have to worry about him making any stupid decisions, like driving when he's been drinking. I love the guy like a brother, but lately, there have been times I wonder what's going through his head.

"So, I'm going to bring Maggie over to Amarre's sometime next week. Erin said to bring you with, and she'll feed us. You in?" I pump the gas pedal a couple of times and crank the engine.

The engine sputters, seems to contemplate giving up the ghost, and then reluctantly turns over. Fickle fucking girl. The sooner Blake takes a look at her, the better.

Chance shifts in his seat and cranks open his window. He slings his arm out into the cold air, catching it in his hand as he stares out into the night. "I don't know. Don't want to infringe," he mumbles.

He's got that look in his eye again, the one that hints at memories better left in the past. His last tour was a maelstrom of shit, and though I was dealing with my own mess and in the process of separating from the navy at the time, I will forever feel like I let him down by not being there for him.

"Not infringing if you were invited, man. And make no mistake, you absolutely were." My words are meant to reassure him, but with Chance, there's never a guarantee on which way things are going to go.

I seriously wish that there was something more I could do for him. I look out for him as much as I can, but the guy is shit with letting people in. *Just like my ex-wife.*

He shifts and fidgets, left hand tapping against his leg as it bounces to whatever song or beat he's got going through his head. Forever moving, dodging and weaving his way through the maze of civilian life.

Chance was the most gung-ho motherfucker on my team—

young and committed to the navy. I had no doubt he'd be a lifer, but what he saw on his last mission, the ones he lost, fucked with him hard.

"We should hit up Jensen, get you some fresh ink," he declares, spinning the conversation in a totally different direction. "It's been so long for you; you're practically a virgin. Gotta bust that cherry all over again."

THREE

Chloe

My desk is clear. The whiteboards are sparkling clean, and the chairs are upside down on the students' desks. Well, all but two of them. I glance at the clock above the door and then check to see if the time differs from that on my phone. It doesn't. And as the hands creep past my meeting time—the one specifically requested by the mom of one of my students—I decide to make the phone call. I don't have another option, and having my parents close to fall back on was one of the perks of moving.

"Hey, Dad. Are you busy?" I ask, dropping my head into my hand.

"Not with anything important, sweetie. What do you need?"

I sigh and suck it up. "I have a meeting with a parent, and she's running late. Can you pick up Jake from after-school childcare? I think this is going to run long, and I can't be late getting him again. They're going to start charging me extra, and

God knows, he's already cranky about having to stay after. He's convinced it's just for babies."

"You got parents complaining about their kids' grades already? You haven't really been there long enough for that, have you?"

"I don't think so... maybe? God, I hope not." Stepping into a classroom midyear isn't easy, but the job was available, and I needed to make the change. I was finally ready to make the change.

"I'll grab him. Maybe take him out for a burger or something." My dad's warm chuckle wraps itself around me.

This is why I moved here. To be closer to my parents. To have a good man in Jake's life. And for help.

After confirming the time and hearing a quick, "I love you," from my father, I scroll through pictures on my phone. Deployments. Reunions. My life with Dallas.

And my heart sits heavy in my chest.

I miss him.

Five years later, almost six, and it still hurts to think about all the things we didn't get to do. All our hopes and dreams. If he'd lived, he'd be close to his twenty-year mark with the army. In my heart, I know Dallas would never consider retirement at first eligibility, but it would have been an option. A full career with time to do something new with his life, maybe enjoy some time together. Deployments are hard, weighing heavy on the framework of the family. Army life is not for the faint of heart.

"Mrs. Triplett? I'm so sorry I'm late. There was a thing at my office and..." Mrs. Amarre drops her bag to the floor and rifles through it, handing me a tissue. She sits on the edge of her chair, a knowing smile on her face, watching as I dab at the tears I didn't notice were gathering on my cheeks. "Are you okay?" she asks.

I force a smile and reach across the desk to shake her hand. "Yes. I'm sorry. I didn't realize I was such a mess."

Her gaze drops to my desk, where a tear rests on the screen of my phone, magnifying Dallas's easy grin. Sadness, pity, or maybe something almost like understanding softens her eyes. "How long has it been?" she asks in a soothing tone.

My mouth presses into a tight line. This is not the reason she's here in my classroom. My display of emotion feels unprofessional. "Five, almost six years."

"Was he active duty? Did you lose him overseas?"

My eyes well up again, and that kind of pisses me off, so I bat away the tears. "He was active, Special Forces. He was stateside, on his way home from the airport post deployment, and he stopped for coffee before our son's kindergarten graduation. There was a robbery, two teenagers, and... he was stabbed and killed. He was so close and just never made it back to us."

The words hurt, even now. The shock of that day, of hearing the news, of how I crumbled. The only things that kept me upright through that mess were the fact that Jake needed me and that I had the support of Jack and the rest of Dallas's team. His brothers.

"Oh, sweetie."

"Yeah, it sucked." I force a smile and try to lighten things.

This long after the fact, I thought I'd be better. Not necessarily over the loss of my husband, but certainly not having panic attacks in gas station convenience stores and crying in front of strangers.

Erin Amarre reaches across the desk and pats my hand. "It's not easy to lose them, no matter how crazy the shit they put us through is. Jesus, the stories I could tell you, but that would require some wine. Maybe a lot of it." She glances over her shoulder at the clock above the door and then back to me. "Do you have any other meetings tonight? Anywhere you need to be?"

I purse my lips and shake my head. "Just chatting with you and then off to my parents' house to pick up my son," I tell her.

She pushes her chair back and stands, throwing her purse over her shoulder. "Good. Let's get out of here and grab a glass of wine. If nothing else, it'll make my kid's crappy math grades easier to handle."

I hesitate but only for a minute because since moving to Virginia from New York, I haven't had a single night out. Not even a glass of wine with a friend. Hell, I haven't really even made any friends here.

With my voice low—because I'm pretty sure the school district wouldn't be cool with this form of parent meeting—I agree, saying, "So much easier." I backpedal when I see concern flashing across Mrs. Amarre's face. "Oh my God, that's not how I meant for that to come out. Tyler will be fine, but wine is never a bad idea."

Somehow, between getting caught crying in my classroom and then implying her kid was a terrible student, Erin Amarre and I became friends. We leave formality behind us and climb into our cars to discuss Tyler and his math grades over wine at her house.

I follow Erin as she winds through town, turning into the driveway of a lovely house right on the beach. Since I don't want to block anyone in, I park on the street between an SUV and a pretty, classic green pickup truck. The polished dark wooden side rails call attention to the beautiful restoration work. This truck is someone's pride and joy.

I follow Erin inside the quiet house, where she pauses just long enough to grab a bottle of wine from the fridge and two long-stem glasses.

Erin leads me out on to her deck overlooking the ocean. It's cool, almost cold, outside, but the setting sun dancing on the water and the low rumble of the waves make it so there is no place I'd rather be.

"You pour, and I'll go grab us some snacks," Erin says, handing me glasses and the wine bottle. "I have a feeling I'm going to need sustenance to get through the bad news."

She slips through the sliding glass door, and I set up our drinks.

It's comfortable out here on the deck. Waves rumble softly in the distance, and saltwater scents the air. I wonder where everyone is. With all those cars out front, it looked like there should be people here.

Erin returns a few minutes later with a cutting board piled high with cheese, crackers, a variety of sausages and meats, and a pile of grapes.

My stomach growls at the sight, and I lean forward in my seat to pluck a piece of prosciutto and some cheese from the board.

With her glass clutched between her palms, Erin rests against the railing and surveys the beach before pausing on a group of guys throwing a ball. "Okay. Looks like they're good for a minute. How underwater on his grades is Tyler? Are we looking at summer school? Is he going to get held back?" She scoots between two patio chairs and lowers herself halfway down before standing again. "He's not going to graduate, is he?"

A laugh huffs its way out of me. "Not necessarily. He can pull up his grade easy enough, but he needs to actually do the work and practice the problems, and then the tests will be a piece of cake."

She quirks a brow at me, finally taking her seat.

"Seriously. I can work with him if you have concerns, but he's just got to put in a little effort. That's all." I shrug and savor the wine. White, crisp. It's a nice change from the full-bodied reds I usually go for. "He's a smart kid. He just needs—"

"Focus? Yeah. I'm going to talk to his coach and see if he can help motivate Tyler." She rolls her eyes and glances back down the beach.

The trio are jogging toward us, tossing an oversize football back and forth between them.

I think about the school newsletter I skimmed through this morning, scrambling to remember what sports were mentioned.

"Tyler's on the baseball team?" That doesn't feel right, but it's the only boys sport I remember reading about.

"No, rugby, and it's not sponsored by the school. Best decision ever though, suggesting he try it," she says before standing to lean over the railing of the deck. She cups her hands around her mouth and yells, "Clark, what's the ruling on grades and playing time?"

Feet thunder up the steps, shaking the deck. I pluck another chunk of cheese and a cracker from the board and pop them into my mouth.

"Grades determine field time. Extra suicides for anything below a B."

The voice delivering the edict skates through me, teasing recognition in the back of my brain, and a shiver runs down my spine. It's familiar, but why? Deep. Smooth.

"Tyler, you heard what Coach said. And Mrs. Triplett is here, too, so there's no weaseling your way out of math home-work. You need to study, practice, and kick ass on your tests. Right, Chloe?" Erin lays it out there for everyone.

A groan filters up the stairs before Tyler lumbers onto the deck. The poor kid has senioritis just like every single other second-semester high school senior.

"Yes, ma'am," Tyler says.

He's a good kid, and he's bright. He just needs to put in the time.

"Hey, Ms. T," he says, politely addressing me with the shortened name most of the boys in class prefer.

"Hi, Tyler." I smile encouragingly at him.

"Blake, Clark, this is Chloe. Tyler's math teacher and the woman in charge of whether he plays or not."

Erin seamlessly switches from hard-ass to loving mom and tips her wineglass at her son. It's funny because while Tyler might be her eighteen-year-old baby, Erin has to take a step back and tilt her head to make eye contact with him. He already towers over her.

Tyler shifts his weight and opens his mouth but stalls. Poor kid looks like he wants to melt through the boards of the deck and disappear. At his first opportunity, he does exactly that, slinking through the patio doors and away from all discussion of his grades.

"The only person responsible for his playing time is Tyler." Blake offers me his hand. "Mrs. Triplett, it's good to meet you."

I shake his hand and wash down my cheese with a quick swallow of wine. "Please, Chloe is fine." Though he didn't say it, there is no doubt in my mind that this is Tyler's father. The resemblance is unquestionable.

The air sizzles around me, almost uncomfortably, but when I take in the man behind Blake Amarre, I'm met with deep chocolate eyes. My cheeks heat as recognition washes over me because the last time I looked into those deep brown eyes, I was flat on my back.

The beautiful man who caught me in my literal fall from grace as we arrived in town is standing before me. My heart kicks into overdrive, and I almost feel light-headed as he approaches. Tall, broad, and with a confident bearing that sends chills down my spine.

"Hi," I say, trying to ignore the zing of warmth spreading from our clasped hands.

The gravelly chuckle he emits doesn't help with the task.

"Miles Kent. You're looking better than the last time I saw you." He does a full once-over, smiling broadly at the confusion painted across my face. Shooting a look at Erin, he clarifies, "Clark is just a nickname."

He accepts a beer from Blake, tilting the bottle to his lips. Each long, thirsty pull sets his throat bobbing as he swallows. His dark stubble hints at a beard in progress. Wind tousles his thick brown hair.

"So, they call you Clark, and your last name is Kent. Really? Do you moonlight as Superman?" I ask.

He could totally pass for the superhero. From what I can see, he's certainly got the body for it. His long-sleeved shirt clings to a solid chest, straining to contain his biceps. And he seems to have found the damsel-in-distress angle in me.

I would love to push his dark hair back from his face, leaving just one sexy curl twisting against his forehead. Another flush of heat singes its way up my chest as my thoughts startle me.

I tried to date a couple years ago, but it was awful. Guilt fought with disinterest, and I decided I wasn't ready yet. I resigned myself to just... not.

Like he can see my thoughts, Miles runs his fingers through his hair. "Could always be worse. I'd have hated hearing Lover Boy whispered in my ear over comms, dick deep in a shitstorm with another guy's hand wrapped around my shoulder." He gives a chin lift to Blake, a small smile tugging at his lips.

Dry. Sarcastic. He speaks my language.

Erin snorts a laugh, and Blake shrugs, saying, "I got no problem with my call sign. I'm secure in my masculinity. You still questioning yours, Clark?"

"Wait, wait, wait. Back up a minute," Erin interrupts, looking back and forth between Miles and me. "You two have met? When did this happen?" She settles into Blake, where he's sprawled on the outdoor love seat next to her.

"Uh, I... Well—"

"Chloe was overcome by her mere proximity to me and fell helplessly into my arms." Miles raises his hand and bows his head in false modesty as he slings his absolutely perfect bullshit version of what happened. "I'm just glad I was there to catch her, soften her fall, and revive her from that fainting spell. I'm used to it," he adds, cocky smirk firmly in place. Catching my shocked expression, he winks and lifts his drink to Blake. "Top that, Lover Boy."

"Oh my God," I mumble and then go on to explain what really happened when we met. Maybe *gloss over* is a better description than *explain* because I sure as hell don't go into details about why I passed out in a convenience store. No one needs to hear about the crazy new teacher's panic attacks.

"Was it low blood sugar?" Erin asks, jumping to her feet.

She pushes the charcuterie board toward me. "Blake, go start the grill, so we can get Chloe fed. We don't need her fainting again."

Blake lights the grill and then follows his wife inside, leaving me alone with Miles.

Miles reaches across me to pluck a selection of cheese and sausage from the board. Muscles bunch and flex beneath a long-sleeved black shirt that seems to be molded to every dip and ridge across his torso and shoulders. "So, tell me, Chloe Triplett, what's your story?" He settles into the seat across from me. Leaning back, he props his ankle on the opposite knee. He slouches low in his seat and drops his snacks in a pile on the flat plane of his stomach before choosing a chunk of cheese and popping it into his mouth.

"My story?" Lord have mercy, I've already shared it once tonight with Erin. I'm not sure I want to do it again.

"Mmhmm. What brings you to Virginia Beach? Where's your little sidekick, and do you always drop like a ton of bricks at the gas station?" He sucks a smear of creamy brie from his thumb and waits for my response.

Nope. Not ready to share. I've just met the man—officially met him. And while dating hasn't actually worked out for me since Dallas died, I'm aware enough to know that a conversation about anxiety and losing the love of my life isn't a great way to test the waters.

And, if I'm being honest with myself, that whole slew of questions was a bit forward.

"I wanted to be closer to my parents. They were sweet enough to take Jake for a bit since I was meeting with Erin, though I should probably go soon and get him." I set my wineglass down and scoot to the edge of my seat, my skirt sliding up higher on my thighs. I shift and tug at the hem.

"Yeah, that's not going to happen. Erin's got it in her head to feed you, so you're going to have to eat before you're allowed to go," Miles says. "It's easier not to fight it."

I hike an eyebrow that gets judiciously ignored.

He pops a stack of cheese slices into his mouth and tips his beer bottle at me to continue talking.

The ocean breeze whips my hair across my face, tickling at my lips. I gather the wild, dark curls to one side and twist it into a loose braid, tucking the ends into the collar of my shirt. It's not a permanent fix, but it'll do to temporarily tame the mess.

I dig my phone from where it sits in the depths of my tote and check the time. I really should go. "I teach high school math at Cox, my parents live inland, and you've met Jake. Oh, and Bronson. You had the pleasure of meeting my dog as well. That's it. That's all there is," I tell him, rifling back through my purse for keys. I desperately need to clean this bag out.

My phone buzzes in my hand with a text from my mom.

"Everything okay?" Miles asks.

"It is." I nod slowly as I read. "My parents fed my kiddo an early dinner and are grabbing some ice cream on their way to bring him home for the night." I tap out a response that I'll be home soon, only to be met with my mother's standard, *No rush.*

I close the Messages app and let my gaze linger on my locked screen. The last picture we ever took together—Dallas, Jake, and me. Bronson is photobombing us over Dallas's shoulder.

It was just before another deployment—"a playdate in the sand," Dallas said.

We had our whole lives left to live. Until his was cut short and my heart was left in tatters.

FOUR

Miles

Whatever has grabbed Chloe's attention on the screen of her phone is not as okay as she would like me to think it is. A hint of sadness clouds her eyes, pulling the corners of her mouth downward. After my world imploded, I've made it a point to be observant as hell, and I have no doubt there's more to her sudden shift than what she's giving me.

"Chloe?"

Her delicate shoulders rise with a deep breath, and she schools her features. "Sorry. Um, I guess I'm fine to stay for a bit." Flipping her frown, a polite smile flashes across her face before settling to a neutral expression. She reaches for her nearly empty wineglass and swirls the pale gold liquid around the bottom, directing all of her focus on it.

With her hair pulled off her face, she's all big blue eyes, thick lashes brushing against her cheeks with each blink. Absently, she pulls at a loose black curl that escaped its confines and tucks it between her lips.

Blake slides the door open, pulling her attention back from wherever her thoughts ran off to.

I pick up the bottle from the table and hold it up to Chloe in question.

She passes me her glass, asking, "What about you, Miles? Are you a native Virginian? Are you on Blake's team? Wife? Kids? Or just hiding in plain sight, ready to swoop in and save the day?"

Wine sloshes into her glass as I stiffen slightly, caught off guard by her questions. Thankfully, Chloe's got her back to Blake because, no matter what the guy thinks, his poker face has gone to shit. He knows how I ended up here and that this was never in my plan.

I huff out a laugh and shake my head, making sure to catch Blake's eye so he knows to lock his shit down. I'm not talking about Aly, about what I had, and how it's no longer mine. We're not going there. "I'm from the Midwest, a small town in—"

"Please tell me you're not from Kansas," she says, mirth dancing in her eyes, all hints of sadness melting away.

Our fingers brush as she takes her wineglass back. Electricity, chemistry—whatever it is, I feel it zinging through me from even the briefest of touches.

"Iowa, but close enough." This isn't the first time I've fielded this question. "And I was a SEAL, but I left the glitz and glamour of that life behind. Fire Born Security has been kind enough to let me keep my superhero status, so now, I get to sit behind a desk and just pretend to be as badass as Blake. All the glory, none of the risk." I nod in Blake's direction.

Thankfully, he just presses his lips together, giving me a tight nod in return. Subject officially closed.

"So, Virginia, by way of Iowa cornfields instead of

Kansas. Do you miss Midwest living?" Chloe asks. "We spent a little bit of time out there before... before settling in New York." As if realizing she said more than she'd wanted to, she brings her wineglass to her lips and turns her gaze out to the ocean.

We. She said *we*, but there's no wedding ring in sight.

So much is not being said in this conversation. Probably more than what's actually being vocalized, and it is way too heavy for dinner with friends. A casual, accidental dinner at that. At least, I hope it's just casual and not a fucking setup.

Blake wouldn't pull something like that, but I wouldn't put it past Erin. She's the one with access to my employee file. She's the one who knows all of my secrets.

"There were other stops along the way," I say, watching her for... what? A tell? Some hint at what she's holding back?

We just met, and I'm already invested. Maybe too invested.

"Life happens whether you're ready for it or not, right?" There's resignation in her words.

Isn't that the truth?

The door slides open, and bowls, plates, and other crap are balanced high in Erin's arms. Tyler follows with more, but when he turns to close the door, he bumps into his mom, sending a bright orange bowl cascading toward the deck. I lunge out of my chair and snag it before it hits the boards.

"Thanks, Clark," Erin says. She obnoxiously bats her lashes and adds, "You're my hero."

Yep. Saving salad with a single lunge. If only everything were that simple.

We fill our plates, and conversation swerves toward safer, lighter subjects. When Chloe's napkin drops onto the plate in her lap, I stand, take her plate, and head into the kitchen. I throw away trash, rinse dishes, and load the dishwasher with as much as I can.

Before I start in on washing what's left, I do a quick check of my phone and see a text from Chance. He laughed and avoided when I reminded him of dinner tonight at the Amarre's. Said he already had plans. Evidently, new ink was preferable to dinner with friends.

Erin's voice drifts in as the door slides open. "Yeah, I get it. But sometimes, you need to ask for help. Jake's too young, and maybe your dad doesn't need to be lifting stuff and climbing ladders, you know? It's no problem to send Blake or Tyler—hell, there's an office full of men at Fire Born. I'm sure we can find some muscle to help out when you need it," Erin offers.

"I'll think about it. Maybe save my phone-a-friend for when something really big happens. Thanks for dinner, the wine, all of it. This was great. I didn't realize how much I'd missed doing things like this. A little adult conversation goes a long way." Chloe smiles when Erin pulls her in for a hug.

"Anytime," Erin says before turning her attention to me. "Miles, stop that. You don't need to be in here, cleaning up."

I drop a few more pieces of silverware into the dishwasher. "No big. You fed me, and Lover Boy helped me out with Maggie. It's the least I can do." I dry my hands on a towel and close the dishwasher door.

Chloe's brows are pinched together, and her head tilts to one side when I meet her gaze. Quick as can be, she looks away and focuses on Erin.

Instead of stopping to think about what that look might have meant, I edge toward the door and add, "I'll grab a few more things from outside and then take off."

I want a minute with Blake, let him know how much I

appreciate his help with my truck. And that if he gets a call to help out a dark-haired math teacher, I'm here for it.

"Don't you dare," Erin says, stopping me in my tracks. "Tyler and Blake can get the rest. Make sure Chloe gets to her car okay, and we'll call it good."

I raise an eyebrow at Erin's nudge. Because by the sly smirk she's sporting, that's exactly what she's doing. Giving me a push that I sure as hell don't need. Hell, I'm not sure I'm even ready for it. But I'm no fool, and Erin throwing her *don't fuck with me* look is all it takes for me to concede.

"Will do. Tell Blake thanks again for me," I say, pulling my keys from my pocket and walking to the front door.

I hold it open for Chloe, and whether I'm ready to move on or not, I can't help but appreciate the way her skirt hugs the curve of her ass as she descends the stairs. And those calves? I don't know how the hell she can walk in those heels, but they are doing the Lord's work, and I send up a silent prayer of thanks.

The lights flash on her vehicle, and at the click of the locks opening, I lengthen my stride, so I'm there to open her car door.

"Thank you." She settles her giant bag on the passenger seat, giving me another nice view of that ass.

She's like fucking pinup art, and I have to bite back a groan and look away before I start popping wood.

Unfortunately, when I lift my gaze, I'm met with a shit-eating grin on Erin's face. I'm busted, bigger than shit, checking out her new best friend. Yep, there's no doubt in my mind that I've been set up.

The front door closes, leaving me standing in the middle of the street, watching this gorgeous woman shift into the driver's seat. She pulls the safety belt across her, clicking it into place.

I'd be lying if I said I don't notice the way the strap hugs her body, nestling into the valley of her chest.

"You good?" I ask, stepping to the side to put the car door between us.

Chloe nods. "Thank you. It was nice meeting you again."

"I had a good time tonight. Drive safe," I say and shut her into the deep red SUV tapping the roof twice in quick succession.

As I step back to watch her drive away, the light of her turn signal flashes way too fast. I wonder if she knows she's got a bulb that needs replacing. For a hot minute, I consider popping back inside and letting Erin know about the failing bulb, but I decide to just go home instead. I can tell her tomorrow at the office.

I crank my vehicle to a start and listen to the engine. Blake knows his shit when it comes to old engines and restorations, picking apart whatever issues might cause a stutter, a cough, or a hiccup. And now that he's stroked Maggie's ego, she's purring in a way I've never been able to get her to. I shoot him a text, thanking him and letting him know about Chloe's taillight, adding in that I'm available to lend a hand if she calls and needs anything.

I slip my truck into gear and take off toward home. Whatever the issue was, Blake worked his magic, and now, she's sliding through her gears like she's eager for it.

Maggie has been the only woman in my life—the only dependable one—for a while. We've spent some serious time together, but she barely even registers in my mind as my thoughts drift back to Chloe and her pinup curves. I don't care what branch of service decorates a man's uniform; pinups and nose art from old World War II planes are where it's at.

By the time I walk through the door of my apartment, I have a ridiculously clear image in my head of Chloe perched on Maggie's hood, looking all kinds of sexy. I should shove the objectifying thoughts away. I really should.

Instead, I shed my sweaty, sandy clothes and climb under the hot spray of the shower. In my mind, her cardigan is busting at the buttons with a flash of red lace peeking through. I picture the way her fitted skirt skimmed every glorious curve, especially the pop of her ass from the lift of her shoes. I squeeze my eyes shut and grip my dick, giving it a firm tug as I imagine sexy-as-fuck seams up the backs of her stockings. I stroke two, three, four more times and then grunt out my release, almost embarrassed with how fast I blew my load. Before I even mentally got her undressed.

With steam swirling around me and hot water sluicing down my body, I finish my shower. I dry off and pull on some athletic shorts.

I grab a water from the kitchen and scoop some ice cream into a coffee cup. *SportsCenter* is already queued up on the TV when I hit the remote. Basketball stats scroll across the bottom of the screen as teams and players are analyzed to death. I pick at my ice cream, trying to make it last but failing miserably. By the time the announcers are done with their predictions on the next handful of basketball games, my cup is empty.

NHL standings lead to baseball chatter, and then I'm done. I shut things down, draining my water bottle at the same time. My dishes clatter as I load them into the dishwasher.

When I finally crawl between the sheets and close my eyes, my brain whirs, picking up speed instead of allowing me to drift off. I'm stuck in this weird place, not entirely single like Chance, not living the family life like I had planned. My ties to my past are holding me captive, not letting me move on. I loved Aly with all my heart, but there's no way I could have stayed with her. Not after what she did.

The next hour is spent trying to shut down my thoughts, but it's useless. I lift my head from the pillow and stare at the drawer next to my bed. The prescription is in there, every single pill accounted for, except one.

My doctor prescribed them for nights like this, where my body is tired but my mind doesn't seem to want to stop. It worked the one time I took it, but I'd rather not do that again. Not now. Not when things have been going so well.

Instead, I turn over onto my back and take that first cleansing breath. I blow it out, completely emptying my lungs, and then slide into the rhythm of box breathing, controlling my emotions. Clearing my mind.

FIVE

Chloe

Anticipation should be reserved for only good things. Vacations. Holidays. Birthdays and peeling back the last little bit of tape when opening presents. It should actually be illegal to feel it for anything other than the good stuff, but more and more, I've been hovering on the edge, waiting for the next battle in this never-ending war.

"It's not a war, Chloe. It's a mission, in-country. A day in the sandbox. A walk downrange. That's all. I'll be back before you know it."

Dallas's words trickle through my mind as I wonder what he would have to say about the elevated tension propelling my car down the road. If he were still alive, none of this would even be an issue. We'd be home on our little farm, surrounded by a couple more kids.

Instead, every muscle in my body is coiled tight. Waiting. Dreading. Preparing for the imminent battle ahead.

"You have your cleats? Water bottle?" I ask Jake as casually as I can, not wanting to poke the beast.

I happen to know for a fact that both items are in the duffel behind my seat. Because I put them there.

Whoever said that boys were easier to raise than girls hasn't met my son.

Jake rolls his eyes, slumps low in his seat, and pouts loudly as he stares at the back of the passenger headrest.

I had no idea eleven-year-old boys could be such nightmares. I miss the days of barely contained excitement, of Jake bouncing on the balls of his feet, of puppy-dog eyes. He had the best puppy-dog eyes.

"This is dumb," he grumbles. "Nobody even watches this stupid sport."

I glance at the dashboard clock as I pull into the first spot at the edge of the field. "Give it a minute, buddy. You might actually enjoy rugby if you just give it a chance. Learn the rules and try. It's good to do something different," I say, infusing enthusiasm into my statement but not too much because, you know, prepubescent attitudes are unpredictable at best.

The click of the cooling engine is the only sound in the car, and what I wouldn't give to have some other noise to distract me or some other person to share this delightful moment with. Not *some* other person. Dallas.

"No."

One, two, three, four...

My jaw works back and forth over my molars.

I count.

I breathe.

I pray for patience and wisdom and just a tiny bit of a reprieve.

"All we did was run last time. We didn't actually *do* anything," Jake whines.

This kid has never been a whiner. Not when he was a baby, not as a toddler. Not even in the first couple of years after we lost his daddy.

"Get your cleats on and buck up, little trooper. It's time to put your game face on and give this a go." I climb out of the car and pray that he listens and does just that, just this once.

The transition from sweet mama's boy to surly tween is a dicey tap dance of uncertainty.

At the back of my car, I pop the hatch and grab the leash neatly coiled in the corner.

"Come on, Bronson. Sit." I point to the edge of the tailgate and rub my hands over the short black fur of his face.

I might get attitude from my kid, but at least the dog still listens to me and gives me the puppy-dog eyes.

I reach to clip his leash on, but like a flash, Bronson takes off in a blur, running across the field.

"Where'd he go?" Jake screeches. Panic peppers his voice because while he might think he's all grown, he's still just a little boy who loves his dog.

"Get your cleats on, and let's go. I'll—" I stop, dumbstruck by what's playing out in front of me.

Jake climbs out of the car and stands next to me, looking as astounded as I feel. "Is he dancing, Mom? Is Bronson dancing like he used to?"

There, in the middle of the field, my dog is jumping and wiggling around the tall, broad stack of muscle. Wide-eyed, I take in the sight, and a gasp catches in my throat. Bronson's not an old dog by any means, just now showing a touch of white on his chin, but he hasn't acted like this in ages. Not since...

"Mom? Why is he doing that now?" Jake appears beside me. "You said he hasn't danced since Dad died." His words are breathed out in a hush.

We stand statue-still as Miles jogs toward us, trying to grab at the worn leather collar that's bouncing all around staying just out of reach because, to Bronson, this is the best game ever. Miles darts his gaze to the cars pulling into the gravel lot, concern pinching at the corners of his eyes. My dog, however, could not care less. His focus is singularly on the man approaching us.

Miles slows, dropping to a knee, and Bronson does a nose-dive, half underneath him. He rolls to his back, twisting as all four paws kick at the air.

"Toss me his leash?" Miles asks, one big hand splayed across the white-and-black dappled chest of the squirming dog, the other extended toward me.

Jake whips the leash from my grasp and runs, practically falling to the ground next to Miles. Other kids spill from arriving cars and run toward their coach, and the now thoroughly exhausted dog who's panting and drooling heavily. Miles clips the leash in place and drops the loop into Jake's hand.

Leaving the new kid on the team to be the center of attention, Miles stands and makes his way to me, Bronson watching him the entire time. "Think your dog might be happier to see me than the kids. 'Course, I'm not going to make him run drills for the next twenty minutes," he says, an easy smile pulling at his lips. He rests a hand on his hip and shifts his weight, swiping at a glistening smear of dog slobber.

"I'm sorry. Here, let me..." I pull the sleeve of my hoodie over my hand and wipe at the mess.

It's not until my hand is firmly attached to his leg that I pause and maybe die a little on the inside because my palm is resting against his thigh. His very muscular, very exposed thigh because those shorts he's wearing are *short.*

My cheeks flame as I pull my hand away like his skin is on fire. The burn of embarrassment simmers up from deep inside me. "Oh, for the love of God," I mumble. "I'm sorry. Really, really sorry. *Jeez.*" I glance around to see just how many people witnessed me molesting the man.

Thankfully, the only one who seems to have noticed is Miles. His easy smile, still in place, is enhanced by a rumbling laugh, rich and smooth like caramel.

"Thanks," he says softly.

I don't know whether to laugh or cry. I just groped my kid's coach. Not intentionally, but still. And to make matters worse, I kind of liked it. I pull my lips between my teeth and bite down on them. Nodding my head, I turn toward the group of boys gathered around Jake and a very pleased-looking Bronson.

"I'm going to take my dog for a walk, I think. Let you get on with your practice." I wave my slobber-stained hand toward the field.

I'm used to being cool, generally full of grace, in awkward situations. Evidently, not today though. Not only is my dog acting like a fool, but I am, too.

I whistle shrilly, drawing attention, and Bronson stands, stretching out his back legs before loping toward me.

A series of sharp claps makes my shoulders jump, and my spine stiffens automatically.

"All right, boys, let's stretch it out like Jake's dog." Miles winks as he passes me, trotting out onto the field.

THE PHONE RINGS a handful of times before Kate answers, laughing and out of breath. "Hey." She can barely get that little word out before gasping for air.

"Tell me I'm not interrupting any shenanigans," I groan.

Kate and her husband, Jack, are the most disgustingly in-love couple ever. I'd hate her if I didn't love her so much.

"*Pfft*, no. Jack's getting the boys settled into a project, and I was just chasing Hays down, trying to get her into some shoes so we can go run some errands." Kate groans, followed by a heavy sigh. "The hell with it. I'm too tired to go anywhere now. Tell me about my first favorite kiddo. How's he adjusting to Southern life?"

Kate was Jake's kindergarten teacher a million years ago. When Dallas's best friend knocked her up and married her, she became family. Dallas would have loved to see Jack and Kate together. To finally see the confirmed bachelor with a family of his own. With five-year-old twin boys and a four-year-old daughter, the sound of exhaustion in my friend's voice is nothing new. But there's something there, something I can't quite put my finger on that hints that there's another one on the way.

Dallas didn't get to see any of it.

Dallas died too soon.

"Jake's adjusting, I guess. He's made a couple of friends." Bronson walks alongside me, his leash folded across his back. "I just need him to be okay, Kate. I need everything to be settled."

"Yeah, I know. And what about you, Chloe? Have you made any friends? Found someone to go out with? Have a glass of wine or maybe dinner?" Kate asks softly. "Maybe someone you want to date?"

Done with our walk, I click the button to open the hatch of my SUV and dump some water into a bowl for Bronson. He drinks thirstily and then lies down next to me as I watch the scrimmage happening on the field.

"I've had some wine," I tell her avoiding that last question she snuck in there.

"And the panic attacks? You've got those under control?"

Jack's voice filters through the background, interrupting, "You tell her yet?"

I laugh. "Tell him I've already figured it out. When are you due?"

Kate groans. "October. I swear to God, I'm going to cut his dick off. I was on the pill and still made him wrap it. It's like he's got super swimmers that'll stop at nothing."

Silence thunders through the distance. I will never wish what happened to my husband on anyone else, but that was supposed to be us. Dallas and I were supposed to have the big family. That was our dream. Reality is such a disappointment.

"I'm sorry, Chloe. I didn't mean—"

"Don't ever apologize for your beautiful life. The sun shining strong on you guys doesn't mean it's dimmer on me. Congratulations, really."

My gaze sweeps over the boys running down the field, tossing the ball like they've been doing this for ages instead of just a couple of weeks. I don't know much about the game, but even Jake looks like he's caught on to things, though he's only just started. Miles runs with them, encouraging both sides in the scrimmage at the same time. He claps his hands, shouting out instructions. When he stops the play, he calls all the boys over to him and pulls two out of the group. Crouching low, he shows them how to grab hold and roll to the ground, tackling in the most controlled alligator roll. His small black shorts pull tight across his ass, the muscles of his thighs pushing the cotton to its limits.

"Chloe, did I lose you?" Kate asks.

She didn't. I heard every word, every encouragement to put myself out there. To allow myself to try. To think about dating. I'm just not sure I'm ready.

"Nope. Sorry, I was watching Jake at rugby practice."

"Rugby? How'd that happen?"

"Hey, it looks like they're wrapping up, so I need to let you go."

"Okay. But you owe me answers. I need to know more about this thing with rugby, and you didn't answer me about maybe dating." Kate laughs.

"Give my love to Jack and the kids, okay? I'll talk to you soon." Not waiting for a reply, I blow a kiss through the phone and end the call. Quick as I can, I reach over the seat for Jake's water bottle.

"Good work, men. That's it for today." Miles's voice booms through the crisp spring air. "Make sure to drink your water and do your moms a favor—shower as soon as you get home."

I will never understand why boys groan the way they do at the thought of taking a shower.

Instead of moping his way back to the car, Jake takes off across the field and gathers up the small orange cones, bringing them to the back of the pretty green truck. Miles lifts a steel bottle to his lips, his throat working as he swallows the water down. My gaze slides over him as I catalog each and every ridge and dip of his well-toned body.

He waves as each kid calls out, "Thanks," or, "Good-bye."

And when Jake presents him with the tower of cones, Miles tucks them in a mesh bag along with several balls. He opens the door to the truck, and Bronson leaps from the back of my SUV and bolts across the lot, hopping into the passenger seat, like it's the only place he belongs.

SIX

A full laugh rumbles out of me. It feels good—maybe a little bit foreign, but good. It's been far too long since I felt this free.

Wind whips through the cab of the truck, ruffling the ears of the hound dog in my passenger seat while he glances out the window, checking out the passing scenery.

Chloe called to him, bribed him with treats. She tried her best, but short of hoisting the seventy-pound dog out of my truck, he wasn't going anywhere.

So, I'm giving Bronson a ride home. At a red light, I pull my phone from where it's wedged under my leg and snap a picture of him. With his black head and his black-and-white coat, he's like the dog version of Chance. Except the dog isn't a dick and doesn't bitch about my truck.

I pull into the driveway behind Chloe's vehicle. The single-garage door lifts, but she stops short of pulling in. Both she and Jake hop out.

"I'm so sorry. I don't know... he's never done anything like this before," she says, talking a mile a minute as soon as her feet hit the ground. She opens the passenger door of my truck and calls, "Come on, Bronson. Let's go."

The dog merely turns his head to me, like we've got some kind of secret understanding. *Don't I wish?*

I swing my door open and step out, the dog following close behind. He trots to the tiny front lawn, lifts his leg, and then winds his way through the garage and into the little white house.

"I don't even know what to say." Chloe tilts her head to the side as she stares through the maze of boxes and crap in the garage to the open door her son and dog disappeared through.

"Don't they say dogs and kids are good judges of character?" I lean against the hood of my truck and cross one ankle over the other. Dirt smudges, from rolling around on the rugby pitch, mar my knees.

"Dogs maybe. Kids"—she shrugs her shoulders—"who knows? Eleven-year-old boys don't seem to use good judgment —ever.

"Thanks for giving my dog a ride all the way home. Can I, um... I feel like I should offer you something in return. Do you have plans for dinner? I was just going to make some tacos." A cloud of uncertainty passes over her face, and she twists her lush pink lips to the side in an adorable pout. She slides a hand behind her neck, fingers toying with the black curls that have escaped from where she's got most of it in a pile on her head.

She's nervous, and I wonder, not for the first time, what her story is. Single mom in a military town is not a big deal. The reasons behind her being alone though, those are vitally important.

"I don't want to impose," I tell her. It's not a *no* exactly.

"It's just a couple of tacos and maybe a cold beer to wash them down. I mean, you did drive out of your way just because my dog decided today was his day to be an asshole. Come on," Chloe says, picking her way through the boxes.

I push a breath out and follow behind her.

As the garage door descends, she turns to me and apologizes, "Sorry for the mess. I really need to find a place for this stuff, but there's always something else to do that sounds so much better."

We step into a bright kitchen with white cabinets and a stone countertop, but half-stripped wallpaper marks the space between the two.

"And you're going to tell me that stripping wallpaper sounds better than getting your vehicle in the garage?" I ask.

This area is safe enough, but it'd be better if she could just pull straight in and close the door, walk right into the house.

Chloe hands me a couple of beers and an opener before pulling what she needs from the fridge. "Yep. Without a doubt. The dirty outside stuff was always the first thing I sloughed off when Dallas got home."

I cock my head, eyebrows high, and thrust an open beer bottle toward her. She rolls her lips between her teeth and then smiles tightly. As she opens her mouth—hopefully to explain, give me something—Jake skids into the kitchen, wet hair plastered to his head, pulling his T-shirt down.

"Is dinner ready yet? Coach Miles, why are you still here?" Jake screws his face up at me while grabbing a sports drink from the fridge.

Chloe cuts open an avocado and squeezes the guts into a bowl. "He's having tacos with us since he had to drive your dog home."

Jake looks from his mom to me and back again and then nods. "'Kay." He paws through the pantry, coming out with a bag of tortilla chips. "Do I have to set the table, or can we eat in front of the TV since it's special?"

"The table, please. And then go do your homework. I'll call you when it's ready," Chloe tells him.

Jake comes off as a typical moody kid more often than not when I've seen him, but tonight, at home with his mom, I get a different picture entirely. He might want to think he's a little badass, but he knows his manners and respects his mother. That says a lot.

He sets the table and scurries off, feet pounding up the stairs.

The heel of Chloe's hand smacks down on the side of a knife, smashing a clove of garlic. She busies herself with chopping stuff and dumping it all into the bowl with the avocado. A squeeze of lemon, a pinch of salt, and a big fucking sigh are all that fills the space between us.

"So, Dallas," I prompt, taking the bowl from Chloe and mixing the contents together.

Silence hangs heavy in the kitchen as she dumps the meat into a skillet. She pushes the ground beef around until it starts to sizzle, filling the air with a delicious scent. "My husband. Jake's dad," she says softly.

My heart screeches to a halt.

This is what I needed to know. I set the bowl on the counter and nod. I check her hand, noting not just the absence of a wedding ring, but also no ridge. No tan line. Not one indication that there's someone else in the picture here.

I seethe. I process. A sardonic laugh huffs its way out of my chest, and as much as I hate what she just said, she said it. It's out there now, and no matter what happy little possibilities have weaseled their way in, I have to do what's right. I need to go. I'm not a cheater—not that anything has happened beyond a handful of conversations and some stray spank-bank thoughts—but if I were this guy Dallas, I'd be fucking pissed that some dick was having dinner with my family. *How did I get this wrong?*

I take a step back, ready to make my excuse and leave, when Chloe continues, "He died—was killed—five and a half years ago. The kicker is, it wasn't a service death. He was on his way home from a deployment." Now that she's talking, the information just flows from her in a torrent.

Relief battles with sorrow as I watch her lay herself wide open.

"Dallas was going to surprise Jake at his kindergarten graduation. Had been planning it from the minute he realized it was even a possibility to make it back from the desert in time. His best friend was on a later flight, but when Jack made it to the school and Dallas still hadn't shown, it never even crossed my mind to worry. I knew his flight had landed. I figured he'd just gotten held up." She slides the pan to a cool burner. "I just didn't realize how close to the truth I was."

A deep, bracing breath lifts her shoulders, and as she releases it, her spine straightens, resolve filling her. "I would love to say that it was completely senseless, but the police report said he saved lives. And that's not something I will ever take away from him. Not ever."

Chloe finishes assembling dinner, putting things in bowls and sliding them across the counter to me. When she finally lifts her gaze to mine, a sad smile pulls at her lips.

Waves of wreckage wash over me, cutting off my air. "I'm

sorry." Anything more than that gets stuck in my throat, choking me. I work my jaw and transfer the bowls from the counter to the small table by the window.

Loss is part of life. Sometimes, it just feels like it's the one thing that can drown me.

Now would probably be a good time for me to share my shit as well. To tell her about Aly and the rest of the story of how I ended up in Virginia. But Jake comes back down to the kitchen looking for his dinner.

So instead of more tragedy, we talk rugby. Chloe asks him about his day, his schoolwork, and plans for the long weekend. He tells me all about his video game, and he seems to really be okay with me being here. I catch him staring at me more than once, but that's it. Nothing hostile appears to be behind it.

Through it all, it never once leaves my mind that this is someone else's family. That they're here because of the love and commitment between two people. Perfect or not, they worked together and found a way to deal with the challenges life had handed them. No one left this union—this thing they had a hand in building—on purpose. Neither of them took what they had and destroyed it. Neither sought to rip a gaping hole in the fabric of their family. Neither intentionally tore this thing apart.

I think I do a pretty solid job of stuffing my shit down and acting like what Chloe just shared with me didn't impact me the way it did. Like it didn't rock my foundation. I smile. I joke. But when Jake says his good nights and scampers off upstairs, I'm about done with myself.

I stack the empty dishes and take them to the sink. I probably just need to cut my losses and go because the last thing I want is for my mood to drag anyone down, least of all this strong, beautiful woman who's already dealt with enough shit.

Chloe sidles up next to me, softly resting her hand on my arm, pinning me in place with a tender touch. The electricity pinging between us doesn't seem to be affected by the black cloud hanging over my head. And despite my Eeyore moment, her touch is like a balm to my wounded soul.

"I feel like I've been slinging one apology after another, but I'm really sorry if that made you uncomfortable." She takes the plates from me and rinses them before stacking everything into the dishwasher. "I don't usually make a big deal out of Dallas's passing, but with the dog and everything..." Her words trail off on the tail end of a shrug.

"It's fine, really. I asked; you answered. That's it. No worries."

Obviously, I didn't do that great of a job at hiding my shit. I grab a wet cloth from the edge of the sink and wipe down the table.

Curiosity digs in, and I ask, "But what does the dog have to do with any of this?"

I clean off the counter as Chloe puts the leftovers in the fridge. Her snort of laughter takes me off guard.

She mutters a quiet, "Shit," and tilts her head back, staring at the ceiling. "Well, Bronson was Dallas's dog. One hundred percent, no doubt about it. The last time I saw him bolt across a field and dance around someone like he did this afternoon, was the last time Dallas came home."

Ice crawls up my spine and settles at the base of my skull.

She chuckles as the fridge door whooshes closed. "And I've never seen him get into a car or truck like that and then flat-out refuse to move."

What the hell?

"I don't know what it means." She throws her hands out to her sides, palms in the air. "I just... I don't know. I don't know why I brought it up. I'm sorry."

My mind races as the past rushes over me, yet my feet seem to be cemented to the floor.

"Miles?"

Hearing my name or maybe the way it spilled from her lips helps to pull my head out of my ass. "This has been a strange-as-hell day for me, Chloe. I'm not gonna lie." Well, maybe I'm lying a little. I don't know.

Other than going silent there for a bit, I'm sure it doesn't look like anything all that strange has gone down. Honest to God, this would be a really good time for me to open up, but I fucking can't. Sure, she shared, but she's obviously had some time to make peace with her loss. Or maybe she's just that much stronger than me on the emotional front.

She chuckles, a little bit husky, completely real. "Yeah. You're not wrong."

"I'm sorry for your loss, really sorry. But I think that needs to be it for apologies. Jesus, I think we've worn them the fuck out. Most overused phrase between us already." I pull my keys from my pocket, and at the metallic jangling, Bronson trots to the front door and wags not just his tail, but also his whole body.

"I'm so—"

"Don't say it. Seriously, don't say it." The lingering tension dissipates minutely with a sigh as we both laugh at the absurdity of the dog. Of the day. All of it. "Thanks for dinner. It was great." I move toward the door, hoping I can get past Bronson without letting him out.

"Might be a good idea to go through the garage," Chloe says under her breath because we're truly at the point where we're dancing around each other, trying to sneak me out without the dog catching on.

I change directions, moving back through the kitchen to the garage, and slip through the door. My arm brushes across her breasts as I do. My lungs squeeze as I weave through the space, holding in a groan.

At the threshold, I turn to take in the clutter. "When you're ready to tackle this, let me know. I'd be happy to help," I offer before my brain catches up to what's coming out of my mouth.

Chloe stands on the step and nods, arms crossed over her chest. Her eyes sweep over the space between us, but she doesn't say a word. Her lips screw up into a sneer, like she would literally rather do anything else than dig into the mess. "Nah. I'll get to it eventually, but it's fine for now." Her sneer turns to a sweet smile as she leans onto the doorframe. "Thank you, though. And thanks for having dinner with us."

I nod my thanks and fold myself into my truck, the headlights illuminating her. This might have been an absolute mindfuck of a day for me, but the sight of her standing there as I back out of the drive is gorgeous. After she finally hits the button and the garage door lowers with her safely tucked away inside, I shove Maggie into gear and drive all four blocks to my apartment.

SEVEN

Chloe

I run my hand through Jake's wild sandy-brown curls, twirling the silky locks around my fingers.

"I wonder if Grandpa would take you to the barber before you guys take off tomorrow," I say absently.

Jake's hair has gotten out of control. It's one hundred percent the color of his dad's, but that curl is all mine.

"Nah, I think I want to grow it out," he says, scooting down on the couch so his head is on my lap.

This is such a weird stage he's in. Tap-dancing back and forth over the line of wanting to grow up but still being a little kid.

"You do, huh?"

"Yeah."

I wind and unwind a curl and tell him, "Grandpa's going to give you a hard time this weekend. You know that, right?"

"Yeah. That's okay. Nonna will shush him and swat at his hand. She's good at that," Jake says. "You're gonna meet us at

Uncle Brent's after dinner, right?" He rolls onto his back, so his big brown eyes, wide and sweet, are looking up at me.

The fights over not taking a shower and the ones over taking too long of a shower seem like they belong to someone else. And for a moment, his hormonal attitude forgotten, he looks like my baby boy.

"That's the plan. I have some meetings I have to go to at school, but then I'll drive up to meet you guys. Why don't you hop into bed, sweets?" A big part of me hates to disturb this precious scene, but the side of me that has to get up early and drag this kiddo out of bed is far more practical.

"Yes, ma'am," he mumbles. Crunching his little body up off my lap, he grimaces and pulls his elbows in tight. The noise that flies out of him belongs more to a man than a boy and sends him off to bed in a fit of giggles. Because let's face it; farts are funny.

I check the locks and turn off the lights as I make my way up the stairs. I peer into Jake's room, and in the few short minutes since he blasted off the couch, he's already slack-faced and lightly snoring.

The dog watches from the guest bed across the hall as I pull Jake's door most of the way closed. I wipe toothpaste from the counter in the hall bathroom, impressed that he at least did a quick brush without being told, and douse the light.

In my bedroom, I softly close the door, leaning my back against it, and sigh. For a short school week, this one has wiped me out. Presidents' Day weekend is a welcome little break. Life has definitely been a lot simpler since moving to Virginia. There's undeniably less upkeep on this house than there was on the farm in New York, but this solo-parenting thing is still not for the faint of heart.

It's a crapshoot whether Jake will bounce out of bed since he doesn't have to actually go to school or if he'll go full-on teenager and want to sleep until noon. The probability of my preferred outcome is not one I'm willing to gamble on, so I pack my bag for the weekend at my brother's house. That's one less thing to worry about in the morning.

On that note, I turn the water on, letting the shower heat up while I grab an old t-shirt to sleep in. One that's so worn the cotton is paper-thin and the unit logo from Dallas's very first assignment is faded to just a ghost of an image.

I peel off my clothes, dropping them on the floor, and step into the steamy bliss. Warmth beats down on my shoulders, the showerhead pulsing water jets into the tight muscles across my back.

The heavy scent of lavender fills the enclosed space as I pour gel onto my shower pouf and let the suds wash over me. I'm not a huge fan of the scent, but one of the other teachers in my department mentioned that it helps her sleep, so I'm willing to try. As I stand under the water, rinsing the bubbles away, I pull the handheld spray from the wall and direct the water down my body.

My thoughts wander to broad shoulders and dirt-smudged thighs as the pulse hits my clit. The image of water sliding over hard-packed muscles, turning dark brown hair almost black, dances through my mind. Heat races through me, and I shudder from a stolen orgasm, hoping and praying that the combination will send me off to dreamland.

The pipes squeal when I turn off the water and reach for my towel. Realization hits me that Dallas wasn't in my mind for the big finish; it was someone new. I dry off, pulling on panties and my shirt. Stuffing my bucket full of guilt down, I turn the bathroom fan on full blast to clear away the steam. Then, I brush my teeth and crawl into bed.

With the hum of the fan providing the perfect white noise, I will myself to relax, to let the soothing scent pull me under. Intentionally focusing on each body part—from my feet to my knees, hips, back, shoulders—I imagine melting into the mattress. I feel that delicious victory of sleep within reach.

The bathroom fan sputters and goes silent. Bronson drops to the floor and pads across the hall to Jake's room. And just like that, every tiny and insignificant noise in the house, all the creaks and groans, amplifies, chasing away all hope of a full night of sleep. I drag myself from bed and flip off the switch for the useless fan, grab my tablet, and sink into an e-book. It might lull me to sleep, or it might keep me up all night for just one more chapter. Who knows?

THE BLARE of my alarm rips me from my dreams, and from the feel of things, I'm pretty sure I have the edge of my tablet imprinted on my cheek from where I fell asleep on it. In the distance, the fridge door rattles closed, and the sound of the TV drifts up the stairs. At least I won't have to fight to get Jake out of bed.

Since I have a full day of meetings and seminars, I dress in skinny jeans and a light sweater. I grab Jake's bag on my way downstairs. Coffee for me, kibble for Bronson, and without much fuss, we are out the door.

I pull into the parking lot of the high school, sliding into the spot next to my mom's car. I'm pretty sure I get the better end of the deal when I trade Jake, his overnight bag and backpack for a bag of doughnuts and another coffee. I'm going to be counting on the caffeine and sugar to get me through the morning.

Team-building exercises follow department meetings, causing the day to drag on endlessly. I swear this is the longest Friday ever, and when the clock finally ticks down to three o'clock, it feels like years have passed. Seasons have come and gone. Continents have shifted.

I race home to pick up Bronson and throw my bag in the car, but as the garage door lifts, water spills down the driveway. A chunk of drywall hangs from the ceiling. Panic rips through me, and I hit Erin's contact on my phone as I rush to pull boxes out of the path of the waterfall.

"Hey, Chloe. Can you hang a sec? I need to—"

I hate how rude I sound, but I cut her off, yelling way louder than is necessary, "There's water pouring through my garage ceiling." I don't know what to do.

"Shit. Okay, hang on. Let me see if Blake can get away."

The line goes dead, and I know I've got to do something. I run into the house, and Bronson passes me, hightailing it right out the door. Obviously, he's been dealing with this catastrophe for longer than he wanted to.

My phone vibrates with a call, and I swipe at the screen, hoping the unknown number is Erin's husband with a quick and easy remedy.

"Chloe, it's Miles. I'm on my way. Have you shut off the water?" The deep timbre of his voice drives me up the stairs toward my bathroom.

"The shower taps are off, but water is still running." Tears sting my eyes. This is the last thing I need.

I barely register the sound of an engine rumbling to life

over the whoosh of my renovation funds flushing down the drain with the endless flow of water.

"The main shutoff. It should be by the water heater. A red lever."

I race back through the house and skid to a stop in front of the water heater. It takes very little effort, but the relief from the halted flow is almost immediate.

"Got it. It's off," I say between heaving breaths, not entirely sure if they're from a little bit of running or a whole lot of panic. "Now, what do I do?"

This isn't supposed to happen. I might have expected it in the old farmhouse when Dallas and I first bought it in New York but not here. Not in this newer house.

"Take a deep breath and grab yourself a beer. I'll be there in ten, and then we'll figure out what we need," Miles says like this is nothing. Then again, it's not really his problem.

Am I even going to be able to get a plumber to show up on a Friday afternoon? I pop the top off the last bottle of craft beer I brought with me in the move.

I make my way out to join the dog on the front step and wait for Miles. Bronson rests his head on my thigh, and I stroke his sleek fur, pushing his ears back. My mind races, bouncing from one thought to the next. I stare at the sunlight dancing through the leaves on the tree shadowing me, bright spots skipping across the grass.

Bronson lifts his head, attention focused down the street. He stands, ambles toward the driveway, and sits. Seconds later, Miles's truck comes into view, causing Bronson to expectantly wag his tail.

Miles steps out of the truck, wearing trim-fit khakis and a dark blue shirt with the sleeves rolled up to his elbows. He pushes his aviators up to rest in his thick brown hair and bends down to greet the crazy-ass dog dancing at his feet.

"You got another one of those?" he asks, eyeing my beer bottle.

"Nope. This is the last," I tell him. I push up to my feet and join him as he takes in the mess in the garage. Soggy cardboard and ruin fill half of the space. "Really wishing I had made time to put all that crap away," I mumble, stopping next to Miles.

"No doubt." He peers up through the busted ceiling, pulling down the hanging chunk of drywall. "What's above here?"

"My bathroom."

"Anything funky been happening in there?"

It's an innocent enough question. Although I'm sure he's referring to pipes and plumbing, my face still heats at the memory of my shower last night.

"Toilet running, pipes clanking?" he adds.

"Um, they squealed last night when I turned the water off after my shower, but I didn't hear anything after that. Didn't see any leaks this morning."

At least, I don't think I did. With my lack of sleep last night and chatting with Jake this morning about visiting his cousins, I was distracted.

I follow Miles up to my bathroom, watching as he looks around.

He opens the access panel in my closet that backs up to the shower. "Yep, busted."

Again, I'm pretty sure he's referring to the pipes, but my brain goes straight to guilty thoughts.

EIGHT

Miles

Every time I ask about Chloe's bathroom, the most beautiful blush pinks her cheeks. I almost want to keep mentioning it, just to see how deep I can get the hue to go.

"I'm going to need to make a run to the store and grab some supplies. Swing by my place to change, pick up my tools. We can get you up and running pretty quick—get the water back on in the house. But fixing the drywall and all of that will take some time. You need to pick up Jake from school, or does he ride the bus?" I glance at my watch, noting that his day should be about over by now.

"He's at my brother's house for the weekend with my mom and dad. I had a professional development day and was planning to drive up there to meet them tonight. That's why when I saw the water gushing, I called Erin instead of my dad," Chloe says, pulling her phone from her pocket. "I need to call and let them know I'm... not coming, I guess."

Words tumble from my mouth before I can stop them. "You go ahead. Just give me a key if you're comfortable with me being here, and I'll work on it this weekend." I don't know what the hell is wrong with me.

I run through a mental to-do list and add, "I should be able to get a good bit of it done and put back together by the time you get home."

The plumbing should be easy enough to fix. If I let things air out, maybe get a couple of blowers, I should have the guts dry enough to start drywalling tomorrow afternoon.

Maybe.

Chloe rolls her eyes at me and shakes her head as her call is picked up. "Mom, hey. No, I'm not on my way. Actually, I'm not going to make it." She goes from talking to her mom to Jake and finally to her dad, explaining over and over again that she's fine and getting things taken care of.

"Yeah, my friend's helping. Jake's rugby coach. Oh, for the love of... Dad, I've got it. Yep. I promise I'll call if I need anything. 'Kay, love you."

I roll my lips between my teeth biting away a smile and shove my hands in my pockets. "So, how long until your dad gets here?" I ask.

Her laugh is so much better than the tears I heard in her voice earlier. "It might just about kill him, but I think we have until early afternoon Sunday. And that's just because my mom won't let him pack them up and come right back home."

It sounds like there's more to it than just that.

"But?"

"But I have to send him pics and promise to call if we run into trouble," she finishes with an eye roll. "I shouldn't complain. This is part of why I moved back to Virginia—so Jake gets to grow up with his grandparents close and my dad doesn't worry about me having to handle everything on my own anymore."

"All right, I'm going to bolt. I'll be back in, like, an hour," I tell her, leading her dog back into the house by his collar.

Chloe digs into her wallet and comes out with a handful of cash. "Here, take this."

She shoves it toward me, but I wave it away.

"We'll square up when we're done."

Jesus, she makes the most adorable little pout as she pops her hip. I'm sure she thinks she's got some badass scowl on her face, but with her lush pink lips pursed and her thick black lashes lowered over those bright blues, she looks sweet and beautiful—not the least bit intimidating.

Back at my apartment, I change my clothes and swap out Maggie for my other truck, loading tools from my garage into the back of the cab. The run to the hardware store takes longer than I hoped, and by the time I'm back at Chloe's house, my stomach is grumbling. I should have grabbed some food for us—a six-pack of beer at the very least.

I back my behemoth up to her garage and start moving shit around. Most of the boxes that were strewn across the garage are sopping wet, the cardboard stinking and disintegrating already. She's got no choice but to go through that stuff now and put it away or throw it.

I unload drywall, a new shower valve, and some other shit, organizing it the best I can. With my tool belt slung over my shoulder, I rap on the door to the kitchen and open it. Sweet hell, there are groceries all over the counter, and Chloe's bent over, pulling a baking dish from the oven, her perfect curves right there for me. I clear my throat. I don't want to scare her, but for the love of fucks, I've got to get my shit under control.

"Hey," she says, straightening up. "I ran to the store while you were gone. Figured the least I can do is feed you. Is lasagna okay?"

"Might be better to ask if lasagna is ever *not* okay." My stomach clings to my spine; I'm so damn hungry. "I'm just going to pop upstairs with my tools, and then I'll be right back." I throw a thumb over my shoulder even though she's not looking.

All the stress of coming home to a flood, and Chloe takes the time to get groceries and feed me.

I take the stairs two at a time and drop my tools on her bathroom floor. I poke my head back into her closet and crank the water shutoff valve. Thankfully, the pipe is damaged above the shutoff here, so it's no big deal to restore water to the rest of the house while I fix the shower. But not until after dinner because the dinner she put together smells better than anything I might have snagged on my way back.

I bypass the kitchen and flip the main water valve back on, relieved that I was right and water isn't spilling through the ceiling again.

"Water's back on," I tell Chloe as I step back into the kitchen.

The perfect *O* of her mouth makes me smile, not to mention the way her eyes blow wide open. She opens the door to the garage, and when she closes it and turns back to face me, we're back to her sexy scowl.

"Why is it not raining in my garage, then?"

"Superpowers," I say, snagging a plate and filling it with food.

Chloe loads her plate and slides a beer in my direction. "I'm so sorry you're wasting your Friday night. Honestly, I'm good since you got the water back on. I can use Jake's bathroom," she rambles. "Seriously, you should go out or whatever."

"I've got a beer and a home-cooked meal. I'm just fine right here."

There's no way I'm going to tell her that my other options include a lonely frozen dinner or grabbing drinks with Chance at Chick's. The bar is fine, but he and I have been there way too much lately. Hell, they might consider putting our names on the deed if we keep up with the pace we've been going.

Flavors burst across my tongue with the first bite, and I can't shovel the food into my mouth fast enough. How long has it been since I had homemade lasagna? It's not something my mom ever made and—

Nope. Not going there.

"So good," I manage to mumble around a mouthful. "Definitely nowhere else I'd rather be." I clear my plate in no time and scoop out a second helping. I check the label on my beer bottle, impressed with her selection. I lean back, a little embarrassed by how quickly I devoured the dinner she made.

"It's local. I didn't know what to get, but the guy at the store said this was close to what I drank at home." Something catches in Chloe's voice when she says *home*, but she shakes her head like she's pushing it away.

"Is that what we had with the tacos? Something you brought down from up north?" Of course, I ask the questions just as her lips close around a big bite of food. I wait as she chews, eyes darting over the freshly tiled backsplash.

She wipes a smudge of sauce from the corner of her mouth and sets her fork on her plate. "Yep. I tried to stock up before the drive down, but there was only so much room for beer in the back of my car with all the other crap I had jammed in there. It's from my favorite brewery in Beekman Hills, the little town we lived in north of New York City."

"Yeah, I'd imagine. How long of a drive was it?" It's ridiculous for me to be concerned about her making that drive by herself.

Chloe hums, scraping her fork through a glob of cheese and sauce and then licking it off. *Does she have any idea what she's doing to me?*

"Seven and a half hours maybe? We packed up before Christmas and drove down to my brother's for the holiday, so I'm kind of guessing. Then, we crashed with my parents until the moving truck showed up." She digs her fork in, cutting another piece and then cutting it in half before finally taking another bite.

"Think you'll go back up? Visit friends?"

"And grab more beer?" she asks, smiling. "Maybe. Jake's other grandparents are up that way, so it'll happen at some point. But, damn, it was a good beer. I've been rationing for two months, trying to make it last."

"You did good, then." I nod toward her renovation project, brows raised, fully impressed. "With that, too."

She glances over her shoulder and turns back to me, setting her half-full plate on the counter. "Why do you look surprised at that?" Her cheeky smile is the cutest thing.

"I'm just saying, you did good." I scrape at the edge of a tile, the tiniest bump of grout that she missed when she wiped it down. "Better than I would have guessed." She scoffs, but I plow forward with a cheeky smile of my own and a wink. "I mean, you didn't shut off the main water valve when you had water pouring through your ceiling. Why wouldn't I be impressed with your tiling job?"

I move around the counter and rinse my plate, setting it in the dishwasher. I could totally eat another full helping, but then I'd need to take a nap, and the shower would never get fixed.

Chloe swats at me as I step around her and asks, "What can I do to help?"

There's enough distraction, just being around Chloe, so I don't need to add to it with having her watch me work.

"Not a thing. Tomorrow, when we dig into the drywall repair, I might need you, but I should be good for now."

I work solo for a bit, music pumping through my earbuds as I swap out the pipe, install a new valve, and replace the old handheld showerhead with a much nicer rainfall fixture. The sleek design looks so much classier and more finished than what she had before.

I open the valves, check for leaks, and gather up my tools. I grab the trash, making sure not to leak water from the hose, and quickly jog down the stairs.

"All set. You want to check out your new shower?" I ask, waggling my eyebrows.

Flirty. Yep, without a doubt, but the last things I expect are the bright red blush and wide eyes when Chloe sees her old showerhead in my hand.

"What did you..." Her gaze bounces from mine to the trash in my hand and back again. She looks absolutely pissed. Or is that embarrassment?

"Shit, I'm sorry. I should have checked with you first. I just thought while I was at it, I'd swap out your old fixture for something new. The other night, you said you were updating, and... Jesus, I totally overstepped this." I did, obviously, but her reaction to the whole thing seems a little off—kind of over the top.

Chloe drops her head into her hands and blows out a very controlled breath. But she doesn't say a word.

"Listen, I shouldn't have messed with your shower. I'm sorry. I'll change them up tomorrow, put the original back."

"No, it's fine. It was on my list of things to do eventually. It just... I was surprised," she says.

"Fine," I mumble. *Fine* is almost always decidedly not fine. In my world, it usually stands for *freaked out, insecure, neurotic,* and *emotional.*

Chloe starts to chuckle, the sound bubbling out of her, and I start to think maybe the acronym is spot-on today.

"I'm well aware of what you're thinking, and I have every right to all the things that *fine* encompasses. Let me see the new one." She runs up the stairs, her footsteps pausing overhead and then tapping lightly back down the stairs. She clears her throat as she steps back into the kitchen. "It's perfect. Thank you."

She takes the old one from me and tosses it in the trash with a smile on her face that, for the life of me, I can't interpret. It's some abstract combination of happy and shy, maybe holding a little bit of secret in it as well.

"Another beer?" she asks.

My beard rasps against my palm as I scrape my hand down my face. I am well and truly fucking perplexed. "It's probably best if I just take off for the night. Get back to it in the morning." I don't know where I went wrong or even if I've fucked up, but now, I'm even second-guessing drywall. The fucking drywall.

"Please don't, Miles. I'm so—shit." She catches herself before the full apology tumbles from her lips. "I'm struggling here. I suck at asking for help, and evidently, I'm just awkward as can be today. Or maybe not just today. Maybe it's more often than I realize."

NINE

I wonder if the earth could just open up already and swallow me whole. Could I possibly be so lucky?

"I stupidly freaked out over every single thing with the bathroom last night. My guilt-ridden, sex-starved brain turned everything Miles said, asked, or did into an over-the-top innuendo. I'm totally channeling my inner twelve-year-old boy," I tell Kate as I hit the button to open the garage door.

I don't know what time Miles is going to come. Come over. Get here. *Jesus.*

I obviously need more coffee. I pad back into the kitchen and pour myself another cup, groaning at the realization that Jake—my sweet, innocent baby boy—is just a year shy of this stage. Unless twelve-year-old-boy humor is the new eleven-year-old-boy humor.

"You don't think Jake knows about sex, do you? God, I need to have *the talk* with him. Fuck me," I whisper-shout into the phone.

Because my luck, timing, and Karma are all out to get me, the door from the garage opens, the doorway filled with a broad, bearded, muscled man. And to make matters worse, it's Jack's voice that echoes through my phone's speaker.

"Want me to do it? If I screw it up with your kid, I should be able to adjust discussion points by the time I need to talk to my boys about dicks and chicks. You're on speakerphone, by the way."

I close my eyes, say a prayer, and do a round of box breathing.

Inhale for a count of four.

Hold.

Exhale for a count of four.

Hold.

When I slide my eyes open, Miles looks like he's fighting hard to hold in his laugh.

"Thanks for that, Jack. You are, too. And now, I need to run. My friend's here to help with the house," I say. "Bye. Love you guys." I tap the screen, ending the call, desperate to keep my embarrassment to a manageable level.

"Good morning," Miles says. He's still trying—and failing—to stuff down a laugh. The way it pushes his cheeks high and lights up his eyes is a good look on him. "How was everything this morning? Enjoy your shower?" Casual as can be, he arches a brow and stuffs his hands into the pockets of his well-worn jeans.

I swear I can feel my blush rising from my chest, up my neck, and flushing my face bright red. Why the interest in my damn shower? He can't know I was thinking about him in there the other night, can he? And if he does know, why the hell would he get rid of my handheld shower? A girl—well, a single mom—only has so much at her fingertips for a quick orgasm on the down-low. God knows, if I had a vibrator hidden away, Jake would find it and ask all the questions.

I drop my head forward, staring very intently at his work boots, because for the love of all things good and holy, I cannot look him in the eye. "It was fine."

He snorts a laugh through his nose and mutters, "Hate that word," under his breath.

"It was great. Perfect. Absolutely no complaints." I lift my coffee mug, desperate for a different focus. "Can I get you a cup?"

"Nah, I'm good. I just wanted to let you know I'm here." He turns back toward the garage and pauses, his fingers drumming against the door. "For what it's worth, Jake probably knows more than you think about sex." He chuckles softly as he disappears through the door.

As the door closes, I stand in the middle of my kitchen, not sure whether I want Miles to be right or utterly wrong. Maybe I should take Jack up on his offer. The guys from Dallas's team swore to me at the funeral that they would do anything I needed. Help in any way. But do I really want a bunch of hard-charging, testosterone-filled, alpha males to explain the birds and the bees to my kid? Probably not.

I know I should go out there with Miles and clean the garage—I can practically smell the mildew from here—but I just can't. I need a minute to tame my embarrassment, so I crank some music and give my house the deep clean that it desperately needs. I'm not sure how it can be as filthy as it is when we've only lived here for a few months. And where do all the lids to the storage containers go? I know for a fact that when I packed things up in New York, I got rid of anything that didn't have a match. Stray lid with no bottom? Gone. Bottom with no matching lid? Out it went. And somehow, it feels like they've not just returned, but also multiplied.

I set to work with the matching game, making myself comfortable on the countertop so I can reach. This is one of the chores I should hand off to Jake. I need some help around here.

A crash echoes in the garage, followed by a loud, "Shit."

I hop down and swing the door open.

Nothing in life could have prepared me for what greets my eyes. *Sweet baby Jesus in a manger.*

Low-slung jeans riding a tad lower due to the heavy tool belt testing gravity. Sweat-slicked muscle packed on top of sweat-slicked muscle, all barely contained beneath a tight gray t-shirt.

My mouth goes dry at the image of male perfection grunting in my garage.

For the first time in ages, I feel like a teenage girl lusting after her crush instead of a single mom. *I can do this. It's okay. Perfectly natural to have thoughts about Miles. To desire... something.*

"Are you all right? I heard a crash," I ask from the threshold.

Miles is standing on a raised platform, arms extended over his head, holding a huge sheet of drywall to the ceiling. A beam of lumber lies to one side, and screws are strewn across the floor.

"Yeah, I'm fine, but can you grab that two-by-four support and shove it up under that end of this sheet?" He nods his head, indicating what he's talking about and where he needs it. He shifts under the awkward weight he's balancing overhead, causing his shirt to lift, showing a hint of dark hair on his tight abs.

I should hurry, move with a little quickness to jump in and help him out, but the flood of lusty hormones seems to slow down my brain.

"Chloe? You gonna help me out here or what?"

"Mmm, yep." I blow out a breath and get my ass in gear. The T-shaped support is heavier than it looks, and I struggle to get it upright and wedged under the sheetrock. "Like this?" I ask.

"Yeah, just grab the base and push it, so it's in there good and tight," Miles grunts out the words.

I know what he means. I know it's innocent enough, and he just needs to make sure the unwieldy thing is fully supported before he lets go. I know all of this, but none of that matters.

My immature sense of humor bubbles back up from where I tried so hard to stuff it down earlier. *Maybe his word choice was on purpose? Maybe we're flirting, and I'm just so out of practice that I'm missing the cues?*

I glance up quickly, and all I see is the pinch of concentration.

I roll my lips between my teeth and bite down, trying hard to act my age.

With a groan, I push at the bottom of the lumber until Miles huffs out, "That's it, right there," and then it's all over for me.

I step back and slip on some scattered screws, falling to the floor. My knee lands smack in the middle of a handful of screws, and pain radiates through my leg. "Shit. Damn it. Ow, ow, ow," I say, half crying, half laughing as I tip over onto my butt.

Miles jumps down from the platform and skates his hands down my back. Across my arms. Barely making contact until his palm meets the knee of my leggings and comes away, smeared with blood.

"Hold still," he says.

He grabs the cotton and pulls. And just like that, my leggings rip, giving way as Miles wrenches the material apart, not stopping until the edge of my panties is exposed. He ignores my gasp of surprise as he whips off his shirt and gently dabs at the broken skin. A stinging pinch, and then the slight burn dissipates as he pours water from a half-empty bottle over the cut. After the aggression with which Miles destroyed my pants, his gentle and delicate touch is almost unexpected.

"Can you bend it?" he asks softly, sliding one hand around my calf and the other up to support my thigh.

How can such big, calloused hands be full of so much care?

"I can," I rasp.

When I try to stand, Miles adjusts his hands, applying pressure to keep me in place. "I asked if you could bend your knee, not if you could stand up."

There's heat in his eyes that reflects my own. He moved me. Kept me where I was, where he wanted me. He manhandled me in the most delicious way.

Our eyes lock as he scoops me up into his arms. He stands, cradling me close to his chest as if it takes no effort at all, and makes his way through the garage and into the kitchen. Feeling the muscles I was ogling earlier bunch and shift against my body has me hot, bothered, and swooning, all at the same time.

Miles sets me on the kitchen counter, placing my injured leg along the breakfast bar. "First aid kit? Need to get this cleaned. Sterilized." The efficiency of his words matches the efficiency of his movements.

"It's in the half bathroom, under the sink," I say, breathless from the way he palms my leg before stepping away. My fingers curl around the edge of the granite, holding on for dear life, because the things I'm feeling right now have me reeling.

Miles returns, clearing a space on the counter, and sets to work, inventorying my kit. "We need to restock this thing," he mumbles half to himself. He scrubs his hands twice over, steam billowing from the faucet. "Need some gloves in here. Better antiseptic that's not past its expiration date." He turns back to me, wedging himself between my thighs, his attention on the blood spilling from my knee. He dabs and blots and then shifts me, so my injured leg spans the sink. He leans into my leg that's hanging off the counter, essentially trapping me there. "Deep breath," he says.

As I fill my lungs, he opens the tap, directing the water at my gaping wound. And if that isn't bad enough, he pulls at the edges of the split skin, opening things up and dousing it, cleaning it even more thoroughly. I whimper pathetically. Tears spring to my eyes, and I start to pant with a bastardized version of Lamaze breathing.

"Almost done. Switch to box breaths. In for four. Hold. Out for four. Hold." He glances up, locking his gaze on mine.

"I know what—" My lips slam shut as he pumps antibacterial soap onto his hands and dribbles the suds over my leg, lighting it up with fire yet again.

"Breathe." He pulls a slow breath in, holds it, and then blows it out through perfectly pursed lips. He nods on the next breath when I match his inhale, completing several rounds of the exercise. "Helps, right? SEALs use that to reduce anxiety and stress." His fingers work deftly, drying my skin, pinching it together, and applying a neat row of butterfly closures. He gathers the trash and throws it all away before washing his hands, and then he leans into the counter next to my foot. "You doing okay?"

His eyes bore into mine, assessing. The deep brown pools pull me in, and once again, my breaths come in shallow pants. His hand slides along the outside of my leg, skimming lightly along my bared skin. He moves forward, following the path his touch maps on my leg, wedging his hips closer to me with each step.

TEN

Chloe's lips are a breath away from mine. Her eyes are hooded, and her chest rises and falls as she sucks in each shallow breath, panting it back out. I slide my hand to her hip, fingertips toying with the tattered edges of her leggings. My other hand threads through the curls at the back of her head.

She gasps as I tilt her head and brush my mouth across hers. Her lips are soft and lush, pliable. The kiss is sweet but scorching. Familiar and, at the same time, exciting and new. For the first time in ages, I feel like I could drown in a woman. Not a woman, *this* woman.

I pull back, just enough to check to see if Chloe is as caught up in this as I am. Her lids flutter open, revealing deep pools of sapphire. Never in my life have I seen eyes like hers. Like the night sky when there's just enough light to give the blackness a tinge of blue. Like the ocean just before the depth sucks all the color away. Truly like the deepest blue gems.

I want her.

I press my mouth to hers and swipe my tongue at the seam, begging for entrance. When her lips part, granting me exactly that, I surge forward, pulling her tight against me. Any space between us is obliterated, incinerated in an explosion of lust and desire.

Her fingers dig into my flesh as she grips my biceps. Hips rock against me, and another whimper escapes her, this one decidedly different from earlier.

Desperate. Needy. Sexy as fuck.

The more she moves against me, the harder my dick gets, straining against the zipper of my jeans. I'm lost in her, caught up in the feel of her writhing against me. Desperate to get even closer to her, I hook my arm around her and pull her body tight against me.

Chloe's yelp of pain is like a bucket of cold water dousing the flames burning hot inside me. I still and ease myself back, gently setting her injured leg back to the counter.

"That wasn't supposed to happen. I'm so sorry. I didn't mean to hurt you." Guilt at, once again, overstepping pushes at the lust pulsing through me.

A breathy laugh huffs between the fingers Chloe presses to her kiss-swollen lips. "Just another weird day. I feel like we're going for some kind of record with those." She plants her hands and pushes herself back from the edge. Away from me.

I don't like the separation. Every cell in my body is screaming for her, reaching for her. Urging me to dive back in and drink her up. But she took space at the first opportunity, and no matter how beautiful, sexy—how fucking alluring—she is, I won't just take from her. Chloe is so much more than a random piece of ass at Chick's or any of the other meat-market bars around.

I wrap my hands around the front of my tool belt. With a little stealth, I make the necessary adjustments to my dick. Sadly, when I glance back up, it's apparent that I'm not nearly as sly as I thought I was.

Chloe's brow is high, and her bottom lip is firmly tucked between her teeth. There's not a damn thing I can say or do to cover up what I was trying to, in fact, cover up. So, I wait. Seconds tick by. My head drops forward until my chin hits my chest. I can be embarrassed, or I can own the fact that I find her attractive. Honestly, it's a compliment. Sort of. *Own it, it is.*

I throw my hands out to the sides, palms up and shrug. "Don't let it scare you. I've got it all under control."

Storage containers and lids litter the counter. A few are scattered on the floor near the trash can.

"Do you need help with this?" I close up her severely lacking first aid kit and pick up the stack of crap I pushed aside.

"Nah, I can put them back. Or just throw them all out and start over. I don't even care at this point."

She pivots and slides to the floor, wincing only slightly as she tests her weight on the injured leg. It hurts to watch her limp gingerly to the pantry, where she bends at the waist, grabbing a folded step stool.

I roll my eyes and quickly stack the containers and lids in the open cabinet, closing the door with a thump. "Put that away. You don't need to be climbing up and down that. You'll pull at the closures and rip it open. In fact, you need to just sit your ass down and elevate that leg." My eyes dart to the living room and then back to Chloe. "You want to settle on the couch, or should I take you up to bed?"

As soon as the words leave my mouth, a smirk pulls at the corner of my mouth. I meant it innocently enough, but the way

Chloe's eyes light up almost makes me chub up again. I could apologize, yet again, but fuck that. If I'm owning shit, I'm going to fucking own it. Besides, there's no denying that her filthy mind is to blame for this mishap.

"I think maybe I'll just sit and grade some papers for a bit?" She says it like a question, like she's asking permission.

"Where do you want to be?" I ask, enunciating each word.

It doesn't matter what she does; she just needs to pick a place and sit. If I'm completely honest with myself, I'd rather have her in the garage with me. Close to me.

Chloe sighs, a lungful of air whooshing from her lungs as she tucks the step stool away. "My bag is by the couch, so I'll just go there," she says, turning and hobbling away, her shredded leggings swinging behind her with each shuffled step.

When she's good and settled, I push back out to the garage and climb up onto the work platform, going back to screwing in the drywall. Thankfully, there's only the one big sheet that needs to be hung. The rest of the repairs are smaller, more manageable pieces that I can handle without the T-support. Taping and mudding the seams is quick and easy. I should be able to sand them late tonight, maybe in the morning.

With the ceiling patched, I clean up my mess and decide to start on organizing Chloe's chaos. I move boxes out to the driveway, laying several on their sides so the waterlogged bottoms can dry.

"What are you up to now?" Chloe asks, stepping down into the cleared-out garage.

The bottom of the box I'm awkwardly carrying gives way, spilling its contents to the ground. Baby clothes, damp and stained, litter the ground around my feet. Cursing, I drop to a crouch and gather what were obviously cherished mementos into my arms.

"I would love to say I'm helping, but my good intent doesn't count for shit when your stuff is blowing in the breeze."

Chloe's face falls at the mess all around my feet. "They're ruined." She hobbles over to me, fingers trembling as she plucks a tiny t-shirt from my hands. The Special Forces shield is emblazoned on the front. Her eyes close as she grasps at the garment and the memories that are attached to it. "Can this weekend get any worse? Seriously. The water, the ceiling falling in. Jake's baby things and God knows what else are ruined in these boxes. My knee is split open, and my fucking showerhead is gone."

She drops the baby shirt and limps back into the kitchen. I can let her sit in there and stew, pissed off and sad. I can, but I won't. I scoop up the shirt she cast aside and add it to the pile in my arms.

Inside, Chloe stands in the middle of the kitchen, bottle of wine tilted upright and her throat working overtime as she drinks straight from it. I toss the clothes into the washer because, with as important as these things seem to her, it's worth a shot to see if we can get the filth and stains out of them.

"Slow down there," I say, taking the now half-empty bottle of wine from her hand.

"Those were Jake's baby things. They were supposed to be passed on—to a sibling, to him when he has kids. And now, they're all ruined." She reaches an arm out, fingers wiggling at the wine bottle. "Give that back."

"Nope," I say, placing it on the counter behind me.

Instead, I coax her back outside with a glass of water and a handful of pretzels to soak up some of the alcohol she just downed, and I dig into the rest of the boxes.

The worst damage was, of course, to the things most precious to her.

"What do you want me to do with these?" I ask, indicating a pile of clothes and uniforms that obviously belonged to her late husband. There's not a lick of damage to any of that stuff.

"I don't know. Maybe it's time to just let it all go. Give it away or..." The wave of sadness that presses down on her is visible from here. "I guess I could ask Jack if there's anywhere I should send Dallas's things. His dress uniforms? Maybe someone else can use them."

"Today's not the day to decide. Those were important enough to move down here. Hang on to them, maybe let Jake decide if he wants them," I say. When I've got everything neatly folded, I set the stacks high on a shelf at the back of the garage. "We'll go get some plastic totes in a bit. Grab some dinner." I break the empty boxes down, load the pile for donations into my truck, and give the floor of the garage a quick sweep.

A couple of plastic totes, a sturdy freestanding shelf, and everything will be organized and tidy, allowing Chloe to safely pull her vehicle into the garage.

"You don't have to do all that. You've done so much for me already." She stands gingerly and fumbles with the camp chair, folding it to store away. "I don't know how to thank you for everything, Miles."

Chloe walks stiffly toward me, and I take the chair from her, tucking it against the wall.

"Do you want to come with me?" I ask. I reach my hand out to steady her if she needs it but hold myself back.

She's moving slow, and I'm sure her knee is tender, but I don't really want to leave her. Not even for a short time. I'd rather have her tucked into my truck beside me with the wind ruffling through her hair.

"Do you mind? I'm not exactly quick on my feet, you know." There it is. Just a hint of her sweet smile. "But I think maybe I'd like to get out of here for a bit. Is that okay?"

"I'd love it." I steer Chloe toward my truck noting that she did at least change out of the leggings I shredded earlier and duck into the house to grab her shoes and purse. My breath catches as I step back out because as many times as I imagined pinup Chloe, dolled up and posed on Maggie's hood, seeing her tucked into the passenger seat—hair wild and not a stitch of makeup, ready to run a couple errands with me—is somehow even better.

As I drive, I itch to reach for her hand.

As we walk through the store, it hurts me to see her pain.

As the sun sets, painting the sky behind her in brilliant colors, my heart feels at peace for the first time in a very long time.

ELEVEN

Chloe

Bronson's ears perk, and he unfolds himself from the couch where he's been sleeping soundly for the past two episodes of my Netflix binge. He slowly approaches the front window, as if he's tracking a bird. It was important to Dallas that his dog be trained for when they had the chance to go hunting.

He stands perfectly still as he looks outside, ears up, tail straight. A barely perceptible tremor running through his body indicates he is prepared to go. All that's needed is the command.

"Bronson," I say sharply as he starts to tremble harder. "Leave it." I push up from the couch and walk to the window to see what has him pointing.

My mom's car is parked across the end of my driveway, blocking Miles's pretty green truck in place. Jake jumps out of the back of the car, trying to look cool but failing miserably. He almost reminds me of Bronson, the barely contained excitement pushing its way to the surface.

The dog wags his stumpy little tail and seems to relax ever so slightly. It only lasts a moment though because the minute Miles steps out of his truck to greet Jake, Bronson loses his mind, whining and dancing his way to the front door and then back to the window. Obviously, I'm not moving fast enough for his liking.

"Bronson, sit," I say firmly.

It's all he can do to obey.

"Stay." I use the hand signal that Dallas taught him to follow as faithfully as he does spoken commands. Keeping my hand to him, palm out, I open the front door and step out onto the front porch.

Bronson whimpers behind me, shaking all over.

"Quiet." Without a thought, I reinforce the command with my pointer finger to my lips, and Bronson is immediately and completely silent.

"Hey. You're back early," I say to my parents as they walk up the drive, nervously darting my gaze to Miles.

Mom rolls her eyes and says, "Your dad was driving us all crazy. Your brother just about kicked us out first thing this morning." She rests her hands on her hips and gives my dad the side-eye.

"The hell he did. Brent was on his way out the door, ready to come down here himself to check and see if Chloe's friend handled her shower issue," my dad huffs. "Who's this?" Dad gives a chin lift toward Miles as he straightens to his full height.

"Miles Kent, sir. I'm the friend." Miles extends his hand to shake and waits patiently as my father sizes him up and waits just a hair past comfortable to accept and shake the offered hand. "Ma'am," Miles says politely to my mother as he offers his hand to her as well.

"It's lovely to meet you, Miles. Eleanor Franks, but please, call me Nora." She holds his hand in both of hers, a smile pulling at her lips as she takes full stock of Miles from head to toe.

My mother turns her sparkling eyes on me, and whatever is about to pass through her lips is going to embarrass me like I'm back in high school and she's meeting my first real crush for the very first time. Not just any crush—Dallas.

"Jake, sweetie, go get your bag from Nonna's car. I'll get you unpacked, so your mama and Miles can show Grandpa what they've been up to this weekend."

Dear sweet Jesus, is this really happening?

I toss my hand out to the side, and my dad doesn't hesitate to lead the way inside, bestowing an ear scratch on Bronson as he does.

"Let's see what you got up to here, Kent," he grumbles.

My mother loops her hand through my arm and smiles slyly as we file into the house after Miles. Of course, she doesn't miss the way Bronson barely contains his shit when Miles stops to greet him.

"Well, isn't that interesting?" she murmurs.

While she might think I'm the only one to hear her comment, the subtle shake of Miles's broad shoulders indicates that he heard not just the words, but also the insinuation in her tone.

I'm torn, not sure whether it's best to run interference with my dad for Miles or face the inquisition by my mother.

Thirty-four years old, and I'm still nervous with a boy in the house, meeting my parents for the first time. A boy with muscles and a cocky grin. A boy with a classic car and capable hands. A boy who makes my heart flutter when I thought for sure it was broken beyond repair. A boy who makes me feel things I never thought I'd feel again.

The decision is made for me when my mom gives me a gentle shove toward the kitchen, saying, "Let's see what we can pull together for a nice lunch, sweetie. We've got some hungry men. Jake, baby, bring that bag in here for me." And just like that, my mama is running the show.

Footsteps creak lightly overhead, the TV buzzes from the living room, and the scream of my mother's silent questions echo in the kitchen. She rummages through my refrigerator, pulling stuff out for sandwiches and salad fixings. We work side by side for a few moments until she can't stand it any longer.

"So..." That single word, hanging in the breeze is all it takes to get me talking, and she knows it.

"Like I told you, Mom, when I got home on Friday to grab Bronson, water was pouring through the garage ceiling. I called my friend Erin, and next thing I knew, Miles was swooping in, taking care of everything."

"Mmm, friend." Her implication rings loud. "And Bronson? He's only greeted one other person that way."

Don't I know it. "Mmhmm," I respond, busying myself with chopping veggies for a big green salad.

"You want to talk about it?"

"Not particularly." I fight the smile threatening to pinch at my cheeks. "He's Jake's rugby coach. He works with my friend Erin. That's it, Mom, nothing more." At least, nothing I'm ready to talk to my mother about.

No matter how good our relationship, she doesn't need to know that the countertop where she's laying out lunch hosted a scorching make-out session just last night. My cheeks flush at the memory of his touch, his lips on mine. The way he moved me and fit so deliciously against me.

"Maybe it's time for more," she says softly. Turning to face me fully, my mother leans against the counter and looks at me, seeing me the way only she can. "Six years, Chloe. Dallas would want you to move on, live your life. He'd want more for you than living with just his memory."

"It's not six yet, Mom, not until this summer. And I know he would. It's just hard to—"

"Mom, is lunch ready? I'm starving. Grandpa wouldn't stop on the way home," Jake complains, bursting into the kitchen. "He said he had to get back and make sure the plumbing was the only thing being taken care of." His words are muffled as he paws through the pantry, but there's no question what my father was hinting at.

If he's okay with saying that to my mom, I don't want to think about what he might be saying to Miles right now.

"Just about, baby. Go yell for Gramps and Miles, okay?"

As soon as his back is turned, I shoot my mom a full *what the hell* look, and bless her, she just laughs and waves a hand through the air. As if that little motion is enough to bat away my annoyance at my dad's comment in the car. Thank God Jake's still oblivious to innuendo. At least, he seems to be.

"Oh, lighten up, sugar. Your dad's just looking out for you."

My quiet call of bullshit is swallowed down as my father's booming voice floats down the stairs along with him.

"That's a fine vehicle out there. You get her that way, or did you put in the work?"

Speaking of thinly veiled double meanings...

Humor laces Miles's polite reply. "Thank you, sir. She was

in rough shape when I found her. Most of the work, I did myself, but I've had to ask for help here and there."

"Well, it looks like you put your heart into her." Respect is evident in my father's words. If only he left it at that, but above all else, he's my dad, and he's not about to miss an opportunity to drive a threat home. "You treat her right, and she'll do the same for you. Just don't jerk her around. Something that special needs to be handled with care. Reverence. You get me?"

"Dad," I warn.

I know he means well, but he's pushing too hard. If he keeps this up, he might end things with Miles before they have a chance to get started.

Thankfully, Miles looks like he's rolling with this display and nods respectfully. "Yes, sir. Loud and clear."

After lunch, I send Jake up to do his homework, and Miles takes my dad out to the garage, so he can inspect the rest of the repairs. I don't know if it's the final inspection or the peek under the hood of Miles's truck, but my dad seems to have been won over.

"Nora, let's go. These kids don't need us old folks hanging around all day. Miles, you ever want to open her up out on the country roads, you give me a call." They shake hands, and then my dad turns to me. "Chloe, your brother missed you this weekend. Might want to give him a call and catch up."

And with that and my promise to see them soon, my parents take off, leaving me with their stamp of approval.

"So, those were my parents," I say, rolling my lips between my teeth. "They mean well, but they can be a bit much."

"They're great. Your dad knows his old cars," Miles comments, smiling. "Hey, how's your knee? Not too sore?"

"It's good," I say, picking up the pile of Jake's freshly

washed clothes and setting it on the stairs. "But I think I'll just wait to take this up when I go later."

MILES CHECKED that everything still looked good on the repairs. He threw the rugby ball with Jake and wore him out. He threw the tennis ball for Bronson and wore him out. And I watched it all from the comfort of my patio chair, my foot propped up on the ottoman. I graded the rest of my papers and updated the online grading system, happy to see that Tyler Amarre was out of danger of summer school. I drank a glass of sangria—fine, two—and I let my mind wander.

I thought of Dallas.

Every couple we knew had had the conversation some-where between deployments. The *what if* conversation.

What if you're hurt?

What if there's an accident?

What if the baby gets sick?

What if something breaks in the house?

What if you don't come back?

We'd had the conversation more than once, and Dallas was adamant that I not pine for him. That I should move on and love again. That finding love and welcoming someone new into our lives wouldn't diminish our love, wouldn't negate what we had.

"Bonus points if he's in the service, extra if he's Special Forces. If he looks like me, we'll call it a tribute—as long as he's good to you and Jake. But for the love of God, don't marry navy or air force. Stick with the army. Soldiers work for a living; navy guys write books and the Zoomies take naps."

I'm sure the other branches of service have similar shit talk about their army brothers, but I've seen the respect, the high esteem they hold for each other.

"I think I'm going to head out. You need anything before I go? Another glass of sangria?" The smooth, deep timbre of Miles's voice pulls me back from the past.

The sun is low, casting pinks and oranges across the sky, a beautiful backdrop for a striking man. A man who looks nothing like Dallas. A former SEAL. Wind kicks up, tousling his dark hair.

"Thank you," I say, squinting up at him.

"No worries. Glad I could help."

I stand, taking my wineglass in hand. I reach for my laptop as Miles steps forward to do the same.

"I've got it." He places his hand on my back, steadying me as he invades my space.

We're close. It would be so easy to slide my hand behind his neck and pull him closer. To tilt my head and kiss him.

His gaze goes soft and drops, settling on my lips.

"Mom, can I have some ice cream?" Jake yells, leaning through the sliding glass door.

The moment is gone in a gust of wind and poor timing. I take a step back and see my disappointment mirrored in Miles's expression.

"Go ahead. Just show some restraint, all right?" I call as Jake disappears inside.

"Yes, ma'am," is echoed between the men on either side of me.

TWELVE

Miles

"Where the hell were you all weekend? You never got back to me."

The smell of stale beer overlaid with Chance's cologne burns my nose. It seems like more and more often, he's showing up at work with the weekend's bad decisions trailing behind him.

I push a bottle of water in his direction and dig through my drawer for some ibuprofen.

"I was helping a friend with some renovations." It's close enough to the truth.

"A friend? What fucking friend is doing house shit and needs your help?" Chance shakes four, maybe five, pills into his palm and washes them down before slumping into the chair across from me. He sets the water bottle on the floor and crosses his arms over his chest. Most likely to hide the way his hands are shaking.

A beat passes, drawing into a full minute, before he lifts his head and fully focuses on me. "That chick, the SOS call Erin got on Friday from her friend. She didn't send Blake in to help, did she?"

My fingers still, hovering above my keyboard. Not that I was actually typing anything of importance, just responding to an email from Aly's lawyer. I shake off his stare. "Blake didn't need to drop what he was doing for everyone. Wasn't a big deal to step in and help her out." I tap the delete button a handful of times and try to think of a stronger way to ask when I actually need to show my face in California.

"Her? Her who? Erin or one of her friends? You got an in with the wives, man? Providing services while their husbands are gone?" A slick look settles on his face.

"Not funny," I say. Yeah, there's a teasing tone, but that's not my thing. Never has been, and sure as fuck is never going to be. Cheating, lying, deception, and avoidance are hard fucking limits. "There's no spouse. You remember that chick who passed out in line at the convenience store when we were out, grabbing lunch, a couple of weeks ago? Turns out, she's Tyler's math teacher. Erin went to school to hash out Tyler's shitty math grade and brought home a new friend."

"Sleeping Beauty?"

"Snow White, man. Get your Disney shit straight. But, yeah, that's her. She had a pipe burst, so I fixed her shower, patched some drywall. No big, just giving her a hand."

"Just a hand?" He scrapes his palm across his three-day stubble, the skin on his wrist shiny with fresh ink.

I shake my head, not wanting to get into this with him. Of course, Chance takes it up a notch, sticking his tongue out between his fingers.

"Shoplifting the pootie? Tapping the single mom? Clark,

that is not like you." He laughs, standing to hopefully walk away. "You're going to have to give up your cape, lose the hero shit. Now that you hit it, man, you have got to quit it. Take a field assignment and get the fuck out of town."

"Right," I say, shaking my head.

I love the guy, but sometimes, I just want to smack the shit out of him. Beat some sense into him. Not because what he's saying is wrong. It's just not even close to what went down, and he should fucking know that's not me.

"Shut up, asshole. I replaced a valve, changed her fucking showerhead, and almost had to take her for stitches after she fell and split her knee open."

As the words spill from my mouth, I know—I just know—he's going to latch on to the comment about roughing up her knees. But, no... Nope, that's not what he goes with.

"Wait, wait, wait, hold up." Heads turn all through the cubicle farm because when Chance is on a roll, people can't help but pay attention. "What kind of showerhead?"

"A nice one. Sleek, clean, modern, brushed nickel. Rainfall—"

"Kiss of death, man. You done fucked up," he says, laughing.

Don't get me wrong; the dude needs to laugh more, but I'd prefer *with* me as opposed to *at* me.

"And you replaced what? Her handheld with the different settings, the pulsing action? Poor girl just lost her best friend, and I'm guessing you didn't even properly console her."

Groaning chuckles and taunting *ooh*s float through the office.

"What? What's the big deal? It was a shitty old showerhead. I definitely gave her an upgrade."

Chance laughs. "You think, but reality is, Superman, you left that woman high and dry. Single ladies—I'm guessing, especially single mommies—have a special relationship with their showerheads. Nothing like pulsing spray on the bean to start the day off just right." A Cheshire cat grin makes him almost unrecognizable. A touch evil and all kinds of shitty. "Taking that away from her, that's just wrong, Clark."

I scoff, "Fuck that noise. Maybe if you were better with your dick or put your mouth to good use, the women you date wouldn't have to get themselves off in the shower."

If—hopefully when—I get there with Chloe, the only reason she'll need a long shower after sex is to wash it all away so I can dirty her up again.

Chance laughs all the way to the door. He just fucking got here, and he's already taking off. "I've got my shit covered, man. No complaints yet." He grabs his crotch, as if that somehow makes his point, and strolls out the door.

I BLOW out a frustrated breath and read the email again. I used to love spring in San Diego. Now, the thought of going back there at all makes me sick to my stomach. I don't really have a choice in the matter, not if I want a shot at justice. Though is justice really even a possibility? There's no way to make any of this right.

Erin needs a heads-up. Jason Grant and Calvin Feuerborn, the owners of Fire Born Security, do, too. I check the project schedule both here and in San Diego. Calvin was instrumental in pushing me out of California, and I don't know if Jason created a spot for me or if there really was an opening, but here

I am. They're the true heroes, the ones who saved me when I was convinced I'd been broken beyond repair.

It's too late in the day to drop this on anyone's desk here, and even though Calvin saw me through the worst of things, I need to follow chain of command. I should work as far ahead as possible, get things set for when I need to bounce, but the thought of why, of what's on the other end of my quick trip, is enough to put me off digging into the next thing on my list.

What I really want is to escape for a minute. Run until I'm exhausted. Drink until I can't remember. Find a little slice of normal.

I lock up my files and shut down my computer. Whatever I need, I'm not going to find it here, in the office at six o'clock on a Thursday night.

"You finally ready to kick out of here?" Chance asks as I pass his desk.

"Yeah, I'm done. You?" I dig my keys out of my pocket as Chance slams his laptop shut.

"Yep. Buy you a drink?"

"I don't know. Probably gonna be shit for company tonight," I say, pushing through the door.

Some people, far more conscientious than me, are still working, so we ignore the flash of the security panel and just listen for the lock to click as the door glides shut.

"One drink. A beer at Chick's, and then I'll let you go fix your shower fuckup." Chance is still laughing as he climbs into his black-on-black-on-black truck, lifted and pristine.

I should go, have a beer, and be done. The problem is, the more I think about my options for distraction, the less I want to be around people. And that right there is the deciding factor for me. I will not give in to the demons that whisper it's best to hide. The evil spirits who lure the vulnerable in with the false promise that it's best to be alone. My choices are drinking with Chance or crashing Chloe's evening. And I'm not ready to share this with her. I need to put the Aly situation to bed. Do what I can to see that my ex-wife gets the help that she needs. And then maybe—just maybe—I can move on.

I pocket my keys and pull myself up into Chance's passenger seat. "Fuck it. Let's get ripped." It's his turn to distract me from my demons.

THIRTEEN

Every time the ref blows the whistle, Miles cringes and rubs at his temples. He holds his own through yelling instructions and encouragement at the players, but it looks like that whistle might be the death of him. The man looks seriously hungover.

"Holy shit, Chloe. I can't believe you're okay with Jake playing this game. It's brutal," Kate says as Jake flings the ball to the player behind him, getting thrown to the ground seconds later.

"It looks worse than it is," Jack mumbles, stalking to the edge of the field. He cups his hands around his mouth and yells, "Let's go, Triplett. Push, push."

I snicker and shake my head. "Is that what he's like in the delivery room?" I pat Kate's baby bump and coo, "Don't worry, baby. Auntie Chloe won't let Daddy yell at your mama like that."

"You don't scare me," Jack tosses over his shoulder at me.

I bark out a laugh. "That right there is some bullshit. I

remember you practically hiding behind Dallas when you wanted to stay in a hotel on leave instead of with us." I let out a low series of chicken clucks.

Jack smirks and fits himself in behind Kate, spreading his hands across her belly. "And it was the best decision I ever made." His sweet declaration is cut off as the ball is tossed to Jake, who runs it in to score.

"Touchdown," Kate cheers as Jack lets loose a shrill whistle.

"Yeah, it's called a try in rugby." I bump Kate with my shoulder, happy just to have her here for a visit. I miss my friends desperately.

When the game is done, Jake bounces over to us, dirty and sweaty and as happy as he can be. "Uncle Jack, did you see that? Did you see me score?"

I love that he still bounces like this when he's excited. It's one of those things I was afraid he'd grow out of before I was ready.

"Aunt Kate, is Hays here? The twins? *Hoe my glob*, are you having *another* baby?" He screws his face up and adds, "Gross," under his breath.

"I am," Kate says at the same time that I scold, "Jacob, what did you say?"

"What? You said I'm not allowed to say *oh my God*, so I changed it." He shrugs and reaches for Jack. "Uncle Jack, you have to come meet my coach, Miles. He's the best, seriously. He fixed Mom's plumbing. And Bronson dances for him, just like he did for Dad." He jogs away from us, Jack trailing behind.

"Well now, he's seen to your plumbing. Is that code or..." Kate might be grinning at me from ear to ear, but the look Jack's throwing me is filled with all kinds of promises to discuss this later.

"Literally, my bathroom plumbing. That's it." I open the back door of my car and spread a towel on Jake's seat. It's not the dirt that concerns me; it's the sweaty-boy smell and my upholstery.

"Oh, he's the one who changed out your handheld. Maybe he needs to make up for that little snafu." She waggles her brows at me and turns toward her husband and Miles sandwiching Jake as they approach. "Sweet mother of God," she says under her breath.

And she's not wrong. Those two broad, badass men flanking my young son are enough to make ovaries explode everywhere.

"Aunt Kate, this is Miles. He's my coach and Mom's plumbing friend."

Jake has got to quit saying that.

"It's an absolute pleasure to meet you, Miles. I've heard so much about you," Kate drawls, letting her Mississippi roots show.

Miles smiles warmly and takes Kate's hand. "Good things, I hope."

"Only the best."

At that, Jack scowls, and I have a sudden urge to buy some hip waders with the way Kate has shit piling up.

"You doing okay?" I ask Miles, shifting closer to him. It's been a few days since I've seen him, and I realize I've missed him.

"Good enough, considering the amount I drank last night. Do you have an extra sports drink or water?"

I rifle through the bag in the back of my car and hand both Miles and Jake plastic bottles.

"You go out drinking like that often?" Jack ask, his brows pulling in tight.

After dealing with my dad and his protectiveness, Miles doesn't seem at all fazed by Jack's interrogation. He shakes his head and drains the sports drink. "No, man. Just went out with my SEAL buddy, Chance. Really wish I had declined and come by Chloe's instead. I definitely would've made a better first impression." He bows his head and chuckles.

"Not another Chance." Kate laughs as Jack mumbles, "Jesus."

Miles cocks a brow and looks to me for an explanation.

"Kate's ex who's now completely out of the closet," I tell Miles. "It only took him three years to tell his parents?" I add and Kate nods her agreement.

"We're going to go get a late lunch, you want to come with us?" I turn to Miles as he eyes the empty bottle in his hand.

He shifts and pushes a hand through his hair. "I think I need to shower and sleep a little," he says, looking embarrassed.

"Come by later, then. We'll be hanging out tonight. Nothing big." Without thinking, I lean up on my toes and brush a kiss on the edge of his mouth.

His warm hand settles on my hip. A throat clears behind me, and when I turn, Kate's smile takes over her face. Jack looks like he could have a stroke. But Jake, his shy smile is the only thing that matters to me.

Miles squeezes my hip once before extending the same hand to Jack. "Great to meet you. Glad you got to see Jake play. Enjoy lunch. I'll catch up with you later, okay?"

ICE RATTLES against the glass as Kate stirs a splash of cranberry juice into her seltzer. She tucks her feet between the cushions of the couch and sighs dramatically. "This really needs a big splash of tequila. And a whole lot less of the seltzer and no cranberry. I just want tequila."

I almost feel bad, sipping on the Paloma she so lovingly crafted for me. Honestly, I think she made it just so she could sniff the ingredients. And maybe lick her fingers.

"Sorry."

"No. No need to apologize. Two years with no Patrón is a small price to pay for..." Kate dismissively waves her hand in the air. "Fuck that, it sucks. I'm going to have to live vicariously through you again, so let's move on to the fun stuff. How big is his dick?"

I blink slowly, sure that my dear, sweet friend did not just ask me that. I glance toward the stairs to make sure that Jake hasn't strolled down for a glass of water, and then to the back door to see that neither Jack nor Miles heard from out on the patio. I suck back my entire drink. The tequila burns, and the grapefruit juice pulls my lips into a serious pucker.

I choke out, "What?"

"Come on, Chloe. The man has been all up in your plumbing, hasn't he?"

"Don't be silly, Kate. No. Just my actual plumbing." My right shoulder pops in a shrug. "He's nice. He just..." My gaze drifts to where he sits outside with Jack. His profile lit by the soft glow of the streetlights behind him. I love that they're talking, getting to know each other. Miles has done a lot for me. The way he's connected with Jake. How he takes care of the little things that, to me, would be huge. "He's a friend."

"A friend you should totally get naked with. I mean, did

you see him in those tiny shorts he was wearing earlier? They barely fit around his thighs, and they sure as hell didn't do much to hide what he's packing." She laughs.

There's nothing I can say to that; she's not wrong. Miles has strong, thick thighs and muscle padding his shoulders and chest. His back tapers in a V that's quite possibly the most delicious thing I've ever seen. It might even be better than the V cut into his hips, but I only caught a hint of that one.

"Chloe? You have—"

"Nope," I tell her crisply.

"Sweetie, I thought you said you were ready. Did something happen to change your mind?" Kate does her best to lean toward me, but she ends up flopping back into the corner of the couch, her hand on her bitty baby bump.

A loud crack sounds as I bite down on an ice cube, my head tilting side to side. "No. It's just been a really long time, you know? And, I've totally been a one-man woman."

"Right," Kate says, nodding. "But you want to, right? The opportunity has presented itself."

"It has."

Jack throws his head back laughing and Miles turns, catching my eye as he smirks.

"And you're ready otherwise? Aside from the nerves about getting back on the horse?"

My brows pop high, and I purse my lips. Miles mimics my expression, and when my gaze flits back to Kate, I don't miss the approving look from Jack.

Light from the screen of Kate's phone casts a soft glow as she taps at the screen. "There. You have a waxing appointment in the morning. We'll take Jake to get doughnuts to celebrate before we hit the road." She taps her screen and then drops her phone to her lap as mine buzzes on the coffee table.

"What the hell, Kate?" I say, glancing at the notification. "Puss 'n' Pits? You scheduled a Brazilian for me at a place called Puss 'n' Pits?"

She pushes to her feet and stretches. "It has great reviews. I'm sure it'll be fine, but life's an adventure, right? How bad can it be?" She snickers as the guys come through the door. "I'm exhausted from growing your spawn. Will you take me to bed?" she asks Jack, batting her lashes.

Jack wastes no time getting to his wife. He threads his fingers through her hair and cups her face reverently. "I would love nothing more," he says, before kissing her soundly, almost embarrassingly. But when Jack fell in love, he fell wholeheartedly. "Miles, it was great talking with you. Chloe, we'll see you in the morning." He shakes hands with Miles and hugs me tight, whispering, "He's a good guy."

Miles and I watch the couple climb the stairs, leaving us alone.

"How was your interrogation?" I ask, leading Miles away from the foot of the stairs.

He steps into my space, crowding me. "I've been through worse, but I'm pretty sure I at least improved on my first impression." His fingers ghost along my skin as he pushes one of my curls off my forehead.

I want him to kiss me. The quick peck this afternoon is not enough.

Miles dips his head, but instead of his lips brushing mine, he sighs. "I think I owe you an apology."

"Why?" That's generally one of those phrases that doesn't

lead to good things, like "It's not you, it's me," or "We should talk."

He bites his bottom lip and stares past me mumbling, "Jesus, this is embarrassing." Finally, he meets my eyes. "I might have screwed up when I fixed your shower. I... uh, shouldn't have assumed that I could just swap out the type of shower fixture without asking. I didn't realize that—"

"Stop." *He is not bringing this up again.*

"People can be very... attached to—"

"Seriously, stop. Please." *Why is he bringing this up again?*

Miles opens his mouth to finish his speech but closes it just as quickly. He props his hands on his hips and exhales through pursed lips. "If you want, I'll change your showerhead back to what you had before." His offer comes out in a rush and I have to laugh to break the tension.

"Maybe, we can promise never to speak of this again. Maybe we can just forget whatever it is that you're trying so hard *not* to say, and I desperately don't want to know who brought to your attention that it might have been an issue."

Miles finally meets my gaze, a heavy haze of embarrassment swirling between us.

"And maybe I'm ready to not rely on a pulsating showerhead so much," I say, though part of me can hardly believe I just said that.

The air between us is all but sparking with attraction and desire.

"I would love to help you in whatever way you need." Miles holds my face between his palms, much like Jack held Kate, and says, "I think I should probably go home now, but when you're ready"—his lips brush mine, softly kissing, gently tasting—"I'm here with you."

I follow Kate up and peek in on Jake. Bronson lifts his head from where he's perched on the end of Jake's bed, exiled from the guest room by actual guests.

With my teeth brushed and face washed, I crawl between the sheets, dreading my morning adventure more than I would a typical waxing appointment.

The next morning, true to her word, Kate and Jack steal my child on the promise of sugar, fat, and carbs.

"I'll bring you one back. A long, thick one, filled with cream," Kate says, her eyebrows dancing.

"Those are Mom's favorites," Jake tosses out.

And I'm thankful once again that he still seems so innocent.

"WELCOME TO PUSS 'N' Pits. I'm Jasmine. I'll be your technician today," the woman behind the desk says softly.

The pale pink walls contrast against black and chrome. The place is cuter than I thought it would be and definitely looks out of place, hosting the curvy bombshell behind the counter. Waves of chestnut hair are rolled back, pinup-style, and colorful tattoos decorate her arms from her wrists, disappearing into the baby-pink scrubs.

"Chloe Triplett? Looks like you didn't complete the forms online, so I just need you to take a minute and fill these in." She slides a clipboard across the counter and smiles broadly.

"Thanks," I say, taking in her long, thick lashes, bright red lips, classic black cat-eye glasses. "I, uh, I wasn't the one who made the appointment." It's a complete mystery to me why I feel the need to share this, but the words just keep tumbling.

"My friend Kate is visiting, and she met my son's rugby coach and my plumbing hero. And then, over drinks, she decided I needed to be ready. Not her drinks though, mine. I was drinking for both of us because she's pregnant with her fourth kid, and I think she feels maybe a little guilty because I was the one who was supposed to be having babies, not her. And now, she's on number four, like I said, and I'm a widow with no reason to even be here." I set the pen across the clipboard and slam my lids shut. I blow out a shaky breath and steal a glance at the poor woman I just unloaded my life on. "Sorry, that was a lot."

Her lips twist into a wry smile, and she reaches for the clipboard. At least I managed to fill in the blanks as I was spilling my tea for the tattooed stranger who's about to get real intimate with just how long it's been for me.

"Sounds like it's been a minute since you've done this." Her voice is oddly soothing, and I relax. At least, as much as one can when they're about to go under the wax spatula and have all the hair ripped from their sensitive bits. "Come on back."

Jasmine leads me to a tiny room and instructs me to undress from the waist down. She presses a button on the wall and speaks into an intercom. The white-framed box is topped with the silhouette of a black cat stretching low over front paws, back arched so its butt is raised, a tail curled high above.

The rest of the art adorning the walls are pictures. Black-and-white images of World War II airplanes contrast with brightly done modern pinups.

"Beautiful," I murmur, though I'm not sure she heard me.

"Jen, babe, can you pop over and watch the front for me? Keely's late again, and I have a client." She doesn't wait for a response but pats the table and tells me to hop up.

The paper on the table crinkles beneath me as she snaps on gloves and stirs the vat of wax, the heavy scent of lavender releasing into the air.

"Dating after loss can be an intimidating thing. Fear, pressure, and guilt can overshadow the excitement and tarnish the shine," Jasmine talks softly and slowly as her hands commit to the torturous task of de-pelting me. The contrast isn't lost on me, but the conversation does what I need it to providing a solid distraction.

"We're not even dating though. Not really." I hold my breath in anticipation of the next swath of wax.

"Mmm, but there's something. A hint, a desire? I mean, I'm all for waxing the kitty for any reason, but I'm guessing there's more to this than just a friend's suggestion." She whispers, "Exhale," before she flicks at the edge of the wax and then pulls one final time.

I wipe at the tear that was inevitable.

"All set," Jasmine says.

With the small bit of privacy afforded me as Jasmine tidies her supplies, I climb off the table and pull on my clothes. "Thank you."

"Sure." She opens the door and ushers me out. "Listen, doesn't matter what your friend thinks, doesn't matter how much time has passed. When the time is right, you'll know it. Just make sure it's on your terms. You need to jump back on that saddle and scratch an itch? Scratch away. But only if you're ready. There's no one-size-fits-all timeline, and God knows, there are plenty of good vibrators out there. Hell, a well-placed showerhead can do wonders for a girl. Right, Jen?"

My steps falter as I enter the reception area. I forgot that anyone else was here, but the last thing I expect is the very tall, very hot, very tatted-up man perched in the delicate pink chair behind the counter.

"You know it, Jaz." The chair groans as he pushes to his feet and plants a chaste kiss to the top of Jasmine's head.

"Wow, I, um..." I stutter, my cheeks flaming at the fact that I'm having this conversation at all, let alone with a strange man right there.

"Sorry. Jensen Bunnsgaard," he says, thrusting his hand out for me in greeting. "Hope the pit-master treated you all right."

"Um, yes?" My voice lifts at the end, making my response more of a question, as the giant Viking of a man's soft hands encase mine in warmth.

"Knock 'em dead." He pats Jasmine's hip, shifting her to the side so he can move past her.

"Your friend took care of everything else online, so have a great day," Jasmine says. I reach for my wallet, but with a wave of her hand, she adds, "She took care of the tip, too, so I'll see you next time. Oh, and, Chloe?"

"Yeah?"

"Jen took the pictures back there—the ones you were commenting on in the treatment room."

My gaze bounces back and forth between them, and Jasmine hands me his business card.

Jensen chuckles, holds the door for me, and tosses a wave over his shoulder as he saunters into the tattoo shop next door. Guns 'n' Bunns, Ink.

FOURTEEN

Miles

In the weeks since we did everything we could *not* to discuss Chloe's shower, she and I have spent more time together. Being with her and Jake is easy. Relaxed. Natural. The look on her face when I told her she should go run errands and Jake and I would have guy time, I thought she'd fall over. I'm not sure why. We're dancing around our attraction to one another and I know for a fact she's caught me staring at her ass more than once. Like now.

"Who knew the thought of going to the grocery store all by myself would hold such appeal?" Bottles rattle in the fridge as Chloe closes the door with a swing of her hip. "Any requests?"

Without looking up from his game, Jake answers, "Cookies, chips. Um, those frozen burrito things and Mountain Dew." His mouth is open, tongue sticking out to the side, as his fingers fly over the controller of his game system.

"Pfft, we'll see. What about you?" She looks up at me from the notepad she's jotting her list on.

She's bent over, elbows resting on the counter, ass looking fucking perfect. The only thing I want is to flip up the little skirt she's got on and run my tongue up the back of her legs. Hell, I'd settle for pushing her hair to the side and nuzzling the back of her neck. She's got me tied up in knots.

"Miles? Anything you want from the store?" Her teeth scrape her lower lip, and her eyes sparkle like she knows exactly what I'm thinking.

"Some beer? Do you have popcorn? Movie snacks?" I lean over the counter next to her, mimicking her pose.

She jots a few more things on the list and then tilts her head, meeting my gaze. "Are you sure this is okay? I can take Jake with me."

I smile and nod. "Take your time. Grab a froufrou coffee drink or something."

"Thank you for this. Really. Just make yourself comfortable, and I'll be back in no time," she says.

I watch as she stands and rips the page off her notepad before sticking the rest of it in the drawer next to the fridge. With her back turned for those few seconds, I grab the pen, add *bouquet of flowers* to the bottom of the list, fold it in half, and then tuck it in her purse.

Chloe grabs her keys and pulls her purse over her head, the strap settling across her body and into the valley of her breasts. She is so fucking beautiful. Classy and sexy when she goes to work. Cute and sexy when she runs around on weekends, doing her errands. Casual and sexy when she hangs out at home. Just fucking sexy.

"Jake, be good for Miles," she calls into the other room. "Text if you think of something else."

As she goes, Chloe trails her fingers across my back and down my arm. She's been reaching for me more. Touches like this, that are sweet, familiar.

Chicken skin breaks out on my legs, and I mumble, "Will do," as she coasts out the door.

I am a lucky bastard that she has welcomed me into their lives so easily, and I need to show her how much that means to me. How much she and Jake mean to me.

I wait for the garage door to rumble down on its tracks and walk into the living room. Jake's perched on the edge of the couch, leaning his whole body, ducking and bobbing along with his avatar on his game.

"All right, bud, finish up whatever mission you're running and then shut it down," I tell him.

"Quest."

"Huh?"

"It's a quest, not a mission. And I have to get the spear of light and then meet up with my guild to save the village." Jake leans sharply to the left and bounces on the cushion before letting out an ear-splitting screech. "Dang it. Now, I have to start all over," he groans.

"Turn it off and take a break."

He slides me a side-eye, challenging me, testing to see if I really mean it.

I do, little man. I absolutely do.

"Come on. We've got shit to do," I tell him. "Get your shoes on and come on out front."

Bronson lifts his head and watches me—I'm sure gauging to see if he's invited to join in on the adventure. It takes longer than it should for Jake to get his shoes on, and by the time he joins me in the front yard, I have the mower on the edge of the lawn, the gas can on the driveway, and am digging through a tote marked *extension cords*, finding everything but.

"Do you know where your mom keeps the cords for the trimmer?" I ask as Jake jumps down the steps.

"Um, in the Christmas bucket. What are we doing?"

Christmas bucket. I guess that makes sense, but why the hell wouldn't she just put it back in with the rest of the extension cords? God love her, she tries to be organized but falls a little short. At least in the garage stuff. Maybe I should have done a more thorough job when I dug into her garage mess after fixing the bathroom, but things were pretty new with us then. Hell, they're still new.

"We're going to mow the lawn, trim the edges. Maybe pull some weeds," I tell him, pulling the tangled orange extension cord out with a sigh. *Why? Why wouldn't she just wind it up before putting it away?* "And we're going to clean this shit and put it away where it belongs."

Jake giggles as he grabs a tennis ball from the corner and bounces it against the wall.

"Why don't you start mowing? I'll straighten this mess and get to edging."

The ball whizzes past, and Jake lunges, missing it. He chases it down and jogs back. "I don't know how," he says matter-of-factly, slamming the ball against the wall again.

I reach out, pulling the ball from midair, and hit the kid with a look that's a cross between disbelief and shock. "Say again?"

He shrugs his shoulders and repeats, "I don't know how. My mom didn't teach me."

I toss the ball to him. "Put that away. It's time for you to learn."

I go over the basics—gas, oil, spark plug. Show him how to prime the engine and start it. What I don't show him is the self-propel lever. Sure, it'd be easier, but Jake needs to get the feel of the mower, respect the power, and figure out how to make a straight row. Besides, the extra effort he expends, pushing that thing across the yard, will wear his ass out. That's something Chloe seems to appreciate. The kid is a bundle of energy.

When I'm satisfied that he's got it, I get back to untangling the extension cord, keeping an eye on Jake. I finish edging the front about the same time he finishes mowing, and we move to the back. He's doing a good enough job, but it's best if I keep an eye on him.

The mower engine sputters and dies, and Jake's a sweaty mess with a smile stretching from one side of his face to the other.

"I did it," he says, looking damn proud of himself.

"You did. Good work. From now on, the job is yours. Every week."

His eyes go wide, and his mouth falls open. "Every week?"

"Yep. Do it without reminders, and I'll give you ten bucks." I should probably clear this with Chloe, but she can't do everything around here by herself. She needs some help.

"Really?"

"Mmhmm. Working hard is one of the rules of being a gentleman, and when you're ready to hit the trimmer, I'll bump you up to fifteen."

Jake pumps his arm in the air in the goofiest fist pump I've ever seen. His gangly legs propel him toward me, and he windmills his arm wide for a high five.

"Jesus. Did you forget your deodorant this morning? You stink, man."

Jake snorts a laugh. "I don't have any."

How does his teacher stand a room full of prepubescent hormone machines and not insist that they use deodorant? Hell, with the way it's warming up during the day, she needs to institute a midday reapply.

I grab the trimmer and wind the cord as I walk toward the house. "Let's go, then. We need to run to the store and get you some."

He zooms past me, zigzagging across the swaying orange cord.

"Get your ass back there and get the mower. The job's not done until your tools are cleaned off and put away. If you're going to do it, do it well and to completion," I say, sharing a nugget of wisdom that my dad handed down to me.

With the grass rinsed away and our tools put up—in the correct places—I close up the house and nod to my truck. "Climb in and buckle up."

I fold myself in and crank the engine. The sun-warmed interior magnifies the sweaty-boy smell.

"Open your window, man. You're ripe." I laugh as he scans the door, confused. I nudge his shoulder with the back of my hand and point to the knob.

Fresh air fills the cabin, blowing his stink out as we work the windows down.

"How come you don't have air-conditioning in this thing?" Jakes asks. He squints against the bright midday sun.

I flip his visor down for him, not that it does much for someone his height, and slide my aviators on. Wind whips through the cab as we gain some speed. I throw my arm up on the open window, the sun blazing down warming my skin.

"Maggie's an old girl, Jake. She's got classic two-forty AC."

Confusion paints Jake's features as he screws his face up at me.

"Two open windows, forty miles per hour."

Over-the-top laughter swirls in the wind, and Jake reaches his arm up to rest on the window. Just like mine.

I wonder, not for the first time, what his dad was like. Would he have taught his son to mow the lawn by now? Taken him to buy deodorant, or would he have just brought it home for him? Would he have had *the talk* by now? Surely, he would have.

I grin at the memory of Chloe's pink cheeks when I walked in on that phone conversation. I should have checked with Jack when he was done grilling me the day we all hung out—see where things sit with that talk. At the very least, I need to check in with her, follow up on it.

Jake follows me into the drugstore. I scan the signs above the aisles and make a beeline for the one we need. Like any kid his age, Jake goes straight to the brand that markets to up-and-coming douche bags.

"This one?" he asks.

"You could choose that one." I rest my hands on my hips and shift my weight.

"That's what my friend has, the *DragonFire* one."

I pluck it from the shelf, and even though the plastic packaging is intact, the scent wafts out. It's almost a hard choice between this stench and the smelly-boy sweat. "Wow, that's…"

Jake wrinkles his nose and moves down the aisle, looking for another option. "What about this one?" He picks a classic.

"You can't go wrong with that one, man."

"How do you know? I can't smell it like that other one."

And that's a good thing.

I grab the matching bottle of body wash from across the aisle and pop the top.

He gives it a sniff and an appreciative nod. "I like it," he says. "It smells like... like you." Jake furrows his brows and thinks for a minute. "Can I get both? The wash stuff too?"

"You know it. Being well groomed—clean and not stinking —is another good rule."

He struts to the cashier, body gel in one hand and deodorant in the other. It's such a small thing, but to him, this is a big moment. A rite of passage.

The cashier takes a step back, and I can't help but laugh.

"That it for you today?" she asks.

"It is. Thanks," I tell her, pulling some cash from my wallet.

"Um, Miles?" Jake bounces to his left and reaches out toward the display of sunglasses. "Can I get some of these?"

I nod, fully expecting him to grab the shiny, mirrored wrap-arounds but when he selects a pair of classic aviators like mine, my heart squeezes. This is how things are supposed to be—but with his dad. And with my kid.

She rings us up and hands the bag to Jake and the change to me. I pull a ten from the stack and hand it to Jake before pock-eting the rest.

"Here you go. Now, you're a man with a job and a classic scent. The girls are going to be all over you at school."

Jake hasn't said anything to me about liking girls, but I figure his first crush can't be too far off, if he hasn't already hit that stage. His face flames red, and his eyes go wide.

"Miles," he grits out through his teeth.

I dig my fingers into my beard, scratching a bit and then straightening out the whiskers. And there we go. It's for sure time someone has a chat with him about girls.

The drive back to the house is silent. Not a word. I half-expect Chloe to be back by the time we get here, but there's no sign of her.

"Why don't you run up and take a shower?" My suggestion is met with more silence.

I thought the silent treatment was reserved for women when everything was *fine*. Guess I was wrong.

I fill Bronson's bowl with fresh water and let him out to do his thing. He trots back in as Chloe pushes into the kitchen, arms laden down with grocery bags.

"Thank you for mowing the lawn. You didn't need to do that, Miles." She drops the bags in a pile and starts unpacking things.

"I didn't. There more in the car?" I ask, already ducking out to scope out her car. I grab the rest of the bags in one hand and the pretty bouquet of flowers tucked off to the side in the other. Chuckling, I hand them to Chloe along with a chaste kiss to her cheek. Closer to her temple really, but it affords me the luxury of burying my nose in her silky black curls.

"These are for you. Hope you like them."

Here I am, thinking I need to volunteer to talk to Jake about the facts of life and what it means to be a man, and I can't even get my ass out to buy flowers for the woman I care about, instead putting it on her grocery list. I deserve a kick in the ass.

"They're my favorites. How did you know?"

I love that she's finally comfortable with giving me shit.

"Is Jake showering? How'd you swing that?"

We work side by side, me putting her purchases away while

Chloe pulls a hunk of meat, potatoes, and some other veggies aside.

"Told him he stunk after he was done mowing. Look, I don't know if I overstepped, but, uh... I took him to the drugstore and got him some deodorant and body wash. He needs it; it's absolutely time."

Chloe stiffens for a second and then cringes adorably. "I've been meaning to do that, but..."

She works some culinary magic, filling the air with the rich smell of meat cooking. It's a tease. One that promises an amazing experience later, but for now, my stomach growls loudly. Chloe hands me a piled-high turkey sandwich from the store's deli department and then turns back to prepping the vegetables.

"But what?"

Her head tilts one way and then the other as she works. "I didn't know how to go about it, if you can believe that. I always figured Dallas would take care of that kind of thing, you know?" She talks about him so easily. I envy that ease. "Did he ask any questions? About, uh... *sex*?"

Much as I want to give her shit about whispering the word *sex*, I'm kind of glad she did. Because Jake comes flying into the kitchen, clad only in athletic shorts, water droplets beading on his bony shoulders.

"Mom, Miles got me deodorant to tame my man smell, and look!" He hoists his arm in the air. "Do you see it? I have pit hair, Mom. Pit. Hair. You gotta look close. See it?" He proudly sidles closer to Chloe.

"Wow," Chloe says with as much enthusiasm as she can muster. "That's... wow."

He drops his arm and digs through the bag still on the

counter, coming out with a smaller turkey sandwich. "I only have it on that side. The other pit is still naked."

Chloe turns, leaning against the counter. She stares intently in the direction that Jake disappeared. Time passes. Too much time, and nerves crawl up my spine. I've faced down shit on missions that didn't rattle me, seen things that have haunted me for many nights after. But overstepping with this family—upsetting Chloe—scares the shit out of me.

Finally, her head bounces in a series of small nods.

I set my sandwich aside. "Are you okay?"

I want to wrap her up in my arms and tell her it's all good, that this is part of watching her son grow up. But she's the one with over a decade of parenting experience. I barely even made it to the starting line of that race.

"I am, but... wow. Mowing the lawn. Pit hair. Man smell? I feel like life happened, and I missed it while grocery shopping."

She leans into me like it's the most natural thing in the world, and I wrap her up, holding her close.

"Do you want me to talk to him? About girls and shit?" I offer, inhaling the scent of her shampoo.

"That's asking a lot of you. It probably goes above and beyond."

"But," I prompt, loving the way she doesn't want to do it herself but can't seem to come out and ask me to do it.

Chloe shifts, leaning back so she can look me in the eyes. "I would be forever grateful, not to have to talk to my son about erections and vaginas and—God help me—masturbation. But that's a big deal. I can see if Jack or one of my brothers..." Concern pinches at the corners of her eyes.

"It's up to you, but I'm here. Jake and I spend time together. I feel like we have a pretty good relationship going."

"Yeah, you do. He likes you, Miles, looks up to you," she says softly, the weight of her words held up for me.

I nod and kiss her, grateful to be included in her family. This is a heavy dose of trust and one that I will happily bear. But when I deepen the kiss and she starts to giggle, I have to pull back. "What?"

"Man smell? Really?"

FIFTEEN

Chloe

"You want me to watch what?" Miles asks. He looks shocked, almost offended by my suggestion.

"*Pride & Prejudice*." I hand him a bowl of popcorn and pull a blanket from the big basket I have next to the couch.

Miles tosses a handful of popcorn in his mouth and stares at me like this is some kind of a joke and he's just waiting for the punch line.

There's no punch line. I am dead serious.

"So, what about *John Wick?* or *We Are Marshall? Gladiator? Man of Steel?* You can't go wrong with Superman."

He smirks as he leans forward to pick up the remote, but I snatch it from the table and flop onto the couch next to him.

"Nope. You said I could pick this one after you and Jake made me sit through freaking Star Wars. And I did. Two hours of my life I'll never get back." I toss the pale blue wool blanket over my legs, bunching it up in my lap. I take the popcorn bowl from Miles's hands and wedge it into place between us. "This movie is so beautiful, I promise. And the time investment will be absolutely worth it." I truly love this movie and particularly this version of it.

Miles groans and sighs through the beginning of the movie, obviously not connecting with the characters and the subtleties of their interactions. "Jesus Christ, what is wrong with these people? Bingley's a twit and needs his ass kicked. Lizzy's mother is a manipulative bitch, and what crawled up Darcy's ass?"

When the popcorn is finished, Miles moves the bowl over to the end table and drains his beer. He sets the bottle into the empty popcorn bowl, and I swear on all that is good at holy, if he hadn't been complaining so loudly through the start of the movie, slamming the characters at every turn, I would've thought his timing was planned down to the wire. But he has complained. He's railed and scoffed the entire time. So, when Miles slouches back into the couch, throws his head back against the cushion, and spreads the fingers of his hand wide, just as Darcy does on-screen, my insides melt. My muscles clench, and desire pools low in my belly.

That scene. That seemingly insignificant action that, in reality, hints at a huge turning point in the story. That right there is what pushes me over the edge. I shove the blanket off my feet and turn to face Miles.

"What?" he asks. And then his strong, beautiful hand flexes again. His eyes dart to the TV and then back to me. He searches my face and asks, "Did I miss something?"

I push up onto my knees and kiss him. He kisses me back, and then he moves his arm around me so that hand is flexing against my hip. Whatever nerves I was harboring, whatever doubts I had about whether this was the right thing to do—the right time—ignite in my burning desire for him. I slide my leg across his lap until I'm straddling him. My legs are spread wide across his massive thighs.

The movie forgotten behind me, I push my fingers through his short, dark hair, gripping his head, taking control and kissing him like my life depends on it. I rock my hips, feeling him harden beneath me.

He slides his hands up my back, pushing my shirt higher until it's bunched up underneath my breasts. Miles pulls away just enough to pull my shirt over my head, leaving me exposed and grinding against him in nothing but thin cotton leggings and my bra.

"Stop, Miles. Stop," I whisper on an exhale.

A pained groan rumbles in the back of his throat as he continues to kiss and lick at my lips. "Why? This movie was finally getting interesting."

On wobbly legs, I stand from the couch and bend over him to grab my shirt from where it landed, hanging over the back cushion.

"God, yes," he mumbles as he pulls me back down to him, burying his face in my cleavage.

A giggle bubbles out of me as his beard tickles my sensitive chest. It turns into a moan as his tongue darts out, and he licks and sucks at first one breast and then the other.

"You have the most beautiful"—*kiss*—"amazing"—*suck*—"bitable tits I've ever seen." He clamps his teeth down on my nipple, through the lace of my bra, and I just about explode.

"No," I moan. "We can't." I force myself to pull away from his touch even though every cell in my body is screaming to get closer.

"Chloe, baby, you're killing me," he groans, reaching into his shorts to adjust his cock.

I take a step back, tugging at his free hand until he stands. We're plunged into darkness when I hit the remote, turning the TV off, and I pull him with me as I walk backward toward the stairs.

"Not here. Not where Jake might walk through," I say, clearing the confusion from Miles's face. "Upstairs. Please," I beg.

Miles pauses at the base of the stairs but only long enough to scoop me up and wrap my legs around his waist. Without making even the slightest of noises, he carries me up the stairs and down the hall to my bedroom. He closes the door behind him, silently flipping the lock. At the edge of my bed, he releases his grip, so I slide down his body, feeling every glorious inch of him along my descent.

He stares into my eyes, my face cradled between his calloused hands. "You're sure? You're ready for this?" His concern for me, the way he treats me as though I'm delicate, something to be treasured, is one of the sexiest things about him.

"Shut up and kiss me."

In the space of a heartbeat, Miles goes from restrained to almost frenzied. Kissing me as he flicks open my bra and tosses it to the floor. His tongue laves a lazy trail between my breasts and down my stomach, dipping into my belly button.

I gasp and squirm as goose bumps pebble my skin.

I giggle and then moan as he curls his fingers into the waistband of my leggings, pulling them and my panties down my legs as he drops to his knees. He kisses the stretch marks that stripe my abdomen. Nips at each of my hip bones and buries his face in my pussy.

I sway and wobble as he pushes my feet apart, granting him access to the most intimate part of me. The place that only one other man has ever known. And as much as I thought sharing that part of me would be hard to do, it's absolutely not.

In fact, the only thought in my mind is, *More, more, more.*

Miles licks and sucks, teasing me with a featherlight touch as his hands roam over my ass and caress my thighs.

"Lie down," he grunts, gently pushing me until I'm cradled in the cloud of my duvet.

He throws one of my legs over his shoulder and worships me with his tongue and hands until my legs start to tremble and an orgasm screams through me, leaving me gasping for breath.

"One," Miles murmurs, crawling up me.

He nuzzles my neck and slides his arm under me, and much the way he's done in the past, he manipulates my body, pulling me up the bed as he moves. He sheds his shorts, pushing them away as if they've offended him.

Our lips press together, hungry for more. Consuming until Miles pulls away, fumbling for his wallet. Finally, he puts the foil wrapper to his mouth and rips, rolling the condom down his length. With both of us protected, he settles his hips between my thighs and cradles my head in the palm of his hand.

Slowly, almost torturously so, he enters me. Rocking gently, bit by bit, until I'm completely and blissfully filled. Miles pauses, fully seated, and hangs his head, each panting exhale blowing a measured puff of breath across my chest.

"Need a second." He forces the words out, almost as if he's in pain.

Unable to hold still, need driving me, I start to rock my hips, pulling a low groan from him. I feel the groan rumble through my chest, his thighs trembling where they're wedged up against the backs of my legs. And then he moves. Filling me, caressing me, kissing me breathless until the pressure builds, spilling over as he swells and pulses in glorious and blissful release.

He covers my mouth with his, swallowing my moan. Hungry kisses calm to lazy caresses of his lips trailing down my jaw and to my neck, where he sucks and nips and soothes.

He holds his weight up, careful not to crush me as I drift back to reality. He places a tender kiss high on my cheek, his lips brushing against my lashes. "Be right back." He rolls away from me and pads to the bathroom, disposing of the condom and washing his hands.

Miles slips back between the sheets, pulling me tight against him. Apparently not close enough though because, after a minute, he rolls to his side, wrapping himself around me. His chest is warm against my back, his arm tucked up under my breasts with his hand gripping my shoulder.

I couldn't feel safer, more contained, more cherished than I do right now.

"Thank you." He presses his face into my hair, rubbing his nose along my scalp as I try desperately to prevent a tear from slipping.

I hold my breath, afraid any movement will send it tumbling down my cheek. The warm drop plummets from the tip of my nose, landing on the back of his hand with an earth-shattering plop.

"Hey," Miles says gently, rolling me to my back. "What's wrong?" Concern laces his words, paints his features, and wraps its way around me. His thumb slides along my cheek, catching another tear as it follows the path already laid out before it. "Chloe, tell me what I've done."

He takes my tears to heart, blaming himself for them without even knowing what's behind them.

"Nothing. I just..."

"Don't shut down. Don't close me out. Did I do something? Push this? Jesus, I thought you were ready, but I... I didn't ask. I just assumed and—"

"No, Miles, no. It's just... I don't know. I waited, maybe too long. Maybe I put too much pressure on myself, and now, it's spilling out in tears. This is..." I pause, rolling my lips between my teeth. There is no good way to bring up another man when I'm lying in Miles's arms. Not when he's just made me feel things I didn't know I was capable of feeling with anyone other than Dallas. "This is the first time since..." I stall again, certain that nothing good will come of this. "There's only been one other man in my life. I... I'm just overwhelmed maybe. Processing. I don't know. Maybe it's just a lifetime of emotion squeezed into the drop of a tear."

His dark brown eyes reflect the scant light filtering through the window blinds. And instead of seeing judgment or even fear at what I just admitted—that this is a big step for me—all I see is reverence. He slides his hand around the back of my neck, cradling my chin with his thumb.

"Oh, Chloe. I don't know if it's the right thing to say, but I am truly honored. Honored to be the man you chose to share yourself with. Honored that you think I'm worthy of you."

"I don't want this though—the emotion, the tears." I swipe at my cheeks, frustrated and embarrassed. I'm stronger than this. I'm not a crier, not really. Not unless it's over something significant, something life changing. And the thought of this falling into that category scares me and thrills me at the same time. "I'm supposed to be happy, swooning over you"—I laugh —"and I am; don't get me wrong. I'm all kinds of swooning. I just didn't expect it with a side of tears. I think I'm broken."

"You're not the broken one, Chloe. You can't be. Not when all you've done is put my useless heart back together."

SIXTEEN

Miles

I drag myself from Chloe's bed minutes before my alarm sounds. God knows, I don't want to go but I promised her I would leave before Jake woke up. After using her bathroom, I rummage around on the floor, pulling my clothes on as I find them, folding hers and setting them on the edge of her dresser.

There's no way I can leave without pressing my lips to hers, not after tasting her. Not after sleeping better than I have in far longer than I want to admit. Dropping to my knees at the side of her bed, I push the curly black mop from her face, the silk-like strands sifting through my fingers.

Chloe wrinkles her nose and purses her lips, settling them into a beautiful pout, one that she would wipe away if she were awake. One that would hover there on the edge of her mouth for a heartbeat until she replaced it with a smile.

I lean forward and feather my lips against hers. More than anything, I want to wake her, and yet I don't. My flight to California leaves at noon, and the pile of work on my desk is higher than I have time to deal with it.

So, I sneak out of Chloe's bedroom, out of her house, and into the dark, silent morning.

It's not until I'm sitting behind Maggie's wheel, my key in the ignition, poised to crank the engine over that I realize there's no way I can pull this off. Maggie's been better since Blake gave her a look, but no way in hell is she reliable enough to get me out of here without drawing attention. I release the clutch and put my back into her. Legs pumping, glutes screaming, I push with everything I have until we're at the end of the block. It might seem like overkill, but when I jump in and crank the engine, the rumble echoes down the quiet street. I was right to take precautions. Hell, I probably would have been better off pushing her the four blocks to my apartment. At least I'd have gotten a workout in.

Thirty minutes later, showered and at my desk, I check into my flight. I should have done it yesterday, but there were more important things to do. Enough time and more than enough energy have gone to Aly. She's taken far more from me than she had a right to.

I clear my head and focus on what's right in front of me. There's no use in getting ahead of myself and borrowing trouble.

"What time did you get in this morning?"

Erin pulls me from the file I've been picking apart. The preliminary breakdown I did on Africa, of course, revealed more issues that need to be addressed in order to move forward.

I glance at the top right of my computer screen and rub my fingertips across my eyes, clearing the fog. "Five, I think." *Is that right?*

The two hours I've spent trying to get ahead this morning have managed to put me further behind with all the shit I've uncovered.

"Jesus, Miles, cut yourself some slack. Don't you leave for San Diego this morning?" The smell of coffee fills the air as Erin tips her travel mug to her lips. "We can move things around, put some other people on this project. You don't have to do it all."

But she's wrong. I do. The compulsion to finish the appraisal, to make sure the assessment is correct and complete—the level of detail exhaustive—is ramped up because of the other fire on my horizon. It's unacceptable to miss even the smallest detail.

"It's no problem. I—" My phone screen lights up with a call from California. At this hour, a call from the West Coast can't be ignored. "Erin, I need to take this." I stand, swipe my phone from my desk, and answer as I walk to one of the conference rooms, shutting the door behind me. "Hey, Ryan. Did I forget to send you my flight details, or—"

"No, no. I got them when I dragged my ass out of bed Saturday morning, but we need to push your trip off," the lawyer says.

Ryan Purdue is the lead on Aly's defense team. I don't know how her parents found him or if they just lucked out, but honestly, I don't think there's a better guy for this case.

"What? Why?" I rake my fingers through my hair.

"Right? Serious kick in the ass, but prosecution is pushing hard for prison time. They've been digging deep, pulling old cases to cite. They want life for her," he explains. "My guess is, they don't understand your angle. It'd make things a whole lot easier on them if you weren't so..." He trails off, struggling to find the right term.

Supportive. Involved. Guilt-ridden. Any of them could apply.

"Jesus Christ, Ryan. I'm the one who should be held responsible. The whole thing is my fucking fault." The conference rooms at Fire Born are soundproof by design, as the shit we tend to discuss around here is sensitive at the very least, but I suck in a calming breath and drop my volume anyway. "I missed all the signs. They were right there, begging for me to notice and I didn't. The blood is on my hands."

Ryan's strained breathing is just barely perceptible, but as seconds tick by, I can't help but check the screen of my phone to see if the call dropped.

"You didn't know, Miles. Aly's doctor, the nurses, if they had no indication, how can you think you should have seen the breadth of her sickness?"

My teeth grind together, my jaw sawing back and forth. "We were married. I lived with her, saw them every fucking day." Emotion clogs my throat.

Ryan's tone softens. In the time we've been working together, he's been almost more of a friend to me than anything. "And why was that? Why were you married to her? Don't forget the depths of her deception. Don't forget what Aly did to make that happen. Your support, the way you stand by her, is commendable. It certainly goes above and beyond. But, Miles, after this round of testimony, I think it's best for you to let it go. Take a step back. You changed your career, moved across the country. It's time to live your life."

My shoulders sag under the weight of his words. The truth in them is raw and painful. "Yeah."

"I'll call when I have something more concrete, date-wise. I'm sorry." Ryan blows out a tight breath and ends the call.

I stand still for a minute, for five, maybe ten. Time seems to spill away as I try to reconcile the things Ryan said with the emotions I have shoved deep down inside.

With three soft raps, the door creaks open just wide enough for Erin's concern to bleed in. "Everything okay?"

I force a tight grin, knowing she'll see right through it. "Not yet, but it'll be fine. I, uh... My trip is postponed, so no need to reassign anything. I just need to cancel my flight, and then I'll jump back in."

Erin doesn't step aside as I approach the door. In fact, she slips through the narrow opening and closes the door behind her. "Why don't you go home? You look exhausted."

I am emotionally wrecked, but I can't. "That's not going to work." I put my hands up, palms out, as she opens her mouth to protest. "I appreciate it, Erin, and I get what you're saying, but I can't just go home and wallow."

"I'm not saying you should wallow, but—"

"I know. I know you're not, but now, more than ever, I need to throw myself into work. Keep my mind on something else." I shake my head and then meet her concerned gaze. "It would kill me to be idle right now."

Concern softens into something closer to understanding, and Erin finally nods. "Okay. But promise me you'll kick out of here early today. Take a nap. Hang out on the beach. Anything. There are much better ways to distract yourself than working a thirteen-hour day on situation analysis."

I shift under her focused attention, uncomfortable with being on the receiving end of what feels way too much like pity.

"We'll see how far I get." With that, I stalk back to my desk, pop in my earbuds, and cancel my travel plans.

ERIN AND RYAN—THEY were both right. I should have left the office at noon, stolen Chloe and Jake from school, and spent the day out here in the sand. Twenty-twenty hindsight and all that.

"Miles, catch," Jake yells, heaving the rugby ball.

His lateral toss is improving. Big-time.

I jog a couple steps forward and pass it back to him. "Now, kick it and see if Bronson can field it." Sand shifts beneath my feet as I walk backward to where Chloe is perched on a blanket. "Are there any cookies left?"

Chloe opens the plastic shell from the grocery store and offers me the last one. "Thanks for this. I don't know what it was about today, but something just felt off, you know?"

I break the chocolate chip cookie in half and hand Chloe a piece as I plop my ass down next to her.

It's a small thing, but I love that she reaches past the piece I offer and takes the smaller chunk, mumbling, "Thanks."

I glance down the beach, checking on Jake's whereabouts, before relaxing into the hand I have propped behind her back. "I do. I hated thinking that I wouldn't see you again for a while. It made sneaking out this morning even worse." I offer a weak smile because I hate sneaking around. I hate anything not fully honest, open, and up-front. Which makes me feel like an even bigger asshole for doing the exact opposite, but I'm not ready. It's too much. Too raw.

Chloe pops the last bite of cookie into her mouth and eyes

me while she chews. Her brows pinch together. "Why wouldn't you have seen me?" she asks.

And it slams me in the face that I didn't even tell her I was leaving town.

Not that I planned on sleeping with her last night, but that would have been pretty shitty to slip out from between her sheets and answer her phone call from the other side of the country. No warning. No explanation.

My beard rasps against my palm as I run my hand down my face. "I was supposed to fly out to California today. My trip got postponed at the last minute, so..."

"Oh. I had no idea."

How would she? I was a schmuck and fucking hid it from her.

"So, you'll go later? For work stuff?"

My hesitance to respond is just enough that she nods once and turns back to look down the beach to where Jake is tossing the ball with some other kid, Bronson running between them. I should suck it up and tell her. Lay out the reasons behind my stellar hangover at the rugby game. Explain why I couldn't hang with her and her friends that night. And just tell her about a cross-country trip that I purposely kept from her.

I'm not proud of the choice, but I don't do any of those things. Instead, I take advantage of the fact that as a former Special Forces wife, she knows there's shit we don't talk about. Things we just can't. I might not be on a SEAL team anymore, but Chloe knows from talking to Erin that we still deal in some hairy shit.

For now, it might be better if she doesn't know what has me in knots. That I lose sleep at night, thinking about all the ways I've failed.

SEVENTEEN

Chloe

There's a code. Elite service members do things, run missions, that keep the world safe, but there's no way in hell the general population needs to know what's going on. Details are a privilege, not a right and certainly not an expectation. Whatever was going to pull Miles away to the other side of the country is obviously not something that I need to know about.

I understand the demands of Special Forces. SEALs. And by extension, even Fire Born Security.

Jake barrels down the beach to where I sit with Miles's arm tucked behind my back, the boy he was throwing ball with abandoned.

"Who was that? Did you make a new friend?"

Obviously, my questions are far too immature for the worldly tween because his eye roll could win awards. Or strain a muscle—whatever.

"Fine. Good job tossing the ball. Nice moves," I add,

changing directions. My body shakes as Miles jostles me with his rumbling laughter.

The insolent child graces us with a huff of a reply, "That was Ben. He's in my class, Mom. *Globrammit.*"

"Nope. Not okay, friend. I don't care how you substitute it. That's still goddammit, and that's just not cool. Try again. Or don't," I add sternly.

Jake kicks at the sand, spraying us. Balling my hands into fists, I give Jake the *mom* look. I've about had it with the hot-and-cold attitude from him, and while I have never been one to wish life away, not even during back-to-back deployments, I can't wait until puberty is in the rearview mirror of life. This is why I teach high school and not middle school.

"I know you have better manners than that," Miles says casually.

Jake blinks, looking from Miles, to me, and back again. I can practically see the wheels turning as he processes just how much trouble he's going to get in.

"Rules of being a gentleman, Jake. I know you know it," Miles prompts.

"Always treat women with respect," Jake replies, his shoulders slumping as he uncomfortably shifts his weight.

"Right." Miles puts his hands out, indicating that he wants the rugby ball. "And were you showing your mother respect just now?"

"No, sir."

I don't know whether to be pissed or impressed, but somewhere along the way, a strong bond has developed between my son and this man. A relationship that was desperately needed. I never sat Jake down and talked to him about dating, about including Miles into our lives. It just happened. Seamlessly.

Naturally. And Jake hasn't pushed back against it at all. It's almost like it was meant to be.

"What are the rules of being a gentleman?" I cock an eyebrow and pull Bronson in to scratch his ears.

Jake stares at where his toes dig into the sand, making deep grooves along the edge of the blanket.

"Wild man?" Miles prompts. "Why don't you get started?" He pats the big white leather ball with his left palm and gently tosses it across me to Jake.

Jake drops the ball to the ground, and recites a handful of life rules, ticking them off on his fingers as he does. I'm amazed. Totally impressed with the things on that list that Miles obviously thinks are important enough to instill in the kids he coaches.

"And the most important one?"

Jake makes a big show of sucking in a huge lungful of air and blowing it out through his nose. His sweet little mouth is pursed, and his brows are pulled low over the chocolate-brown eyes he got from his father. "Always mind your manners, and above all else, be a gentleman," he says.

A broad smile stretches across Miles's face, pride evident. "Nicely done."

He holds his hand out for Jake to toss the ball back to him. And when Jake holds off, tossing the ball between his hands, Miles hops to his feet with a growl, sending Jake running as fast as his little legs can take him. The sand makes it a challenge, so it takes nothing for Miles to be within reach.

Miles taps at the ball, zigzagging around Jake, chasing him, and playing. *Playing.* Of all things, who would think that such a simple thing as a boy playing ball, laughing wholeheartedly, would be such an amazing sight to behold?

I gather our trash and carefully fold the blanket, shaking out the sand. And then I just stand. The sun-warmed sand shifting beneath my feet as the cool evening breeze swirls my hair around my head in an unruly black cloud. Peace wraps me up, not just from seeing the carefree way my kiddo is laughing and playing and thoroughly enjoying life, but also from seeing that reflected in Miles as well.

"Come on, Bronson," I call, throwing the blanket over one arm and grabbing the bag of trash in the other.

Miles and Jake trot toward me, the rugby ball flying back and forth between them as they run.

"Mom, can Miles and I go get ice cream?" Sweat plasters sandy-brown curls to Jake's temple.

"Just you and Miles? I don't get any?" I huff out a laugh.

"You don't even like ice cream," Jake says, his lip popping up in a sneer.

Concern, maybe confusion, clouds Miles's face. He props his hands low on his hips and looks at me like I'm insane. It's not the first time I've gotten that look over this. "You don't like ice cream? Is that a thing?"

"She's weird, right?"

I toss the trash into a nearby can and click the locks open on my car. Miles reaches forward to open the back hatch, tapping the bumper for Bronson to hop in. He takes the blanket from me, giving it a final shake before tucking it in the back.

"I don't know about weird. But she's definitely one of a kind."

Electricity skitters up my spine as Miles's hand gently guides me to the driver's side. He opens the door for me, holding it until I'm settled.

"A single scoop, I promise. Then, I'll drop him home and head out."

"You can hang with us for a bit if you want. Maybe make a beer float. Watch a movie or something?"

"You don't mind?"

A laugh bubbles up, escaping through my nose. "No. I would love to watch another movie with you." I wink, giddy at the huge smile that lights up his eyes.

With a quick nod, Miles closes my car door and calls to Jake, "That's how it's done, my friend. It's never the wrong thing to do—"

"To open a door for a lady," Jake finishes. "I *know*. Can we just go now?"

I roll down my windows and yell, "See you at home," as I take off out of the parking lot.

"WHAT'S YOUR SECRET?" I ask Miles as he pulls my feet onto his lap.

He chuckles as a moan settles deep in my chest. His thumb pushes into the arch of my foot, a warm palm wrapped around my calf. It's intimate but so comfortable, like we've been doing this forever.

"I dazzle you with my good looks, manly muscles, and sparkling personality," he replies. "If it all goes to plan, I get to carry you upstairs again tonight and fall asleep to the sound of you snoring."

I dig my toes into his side, hitting a tickle spot on the first try, making Miles jump. His hand wraps around my ankle, and my ass slides across the cushion as he pulls me toward him.

There is something so amazingly sexy about the way he moves me. On more than one occasion, Miles has used a minimal amount of effort to manipulate my body, putting me where he wants me. Not in a forceful way, always gentle. Always with respect. And always to my benefit.

"That goes without saying."

"It does?" he asks, his hands roaming up my leg, kneading the taut muscles in my calves.

I dig my other foot into his side, and when he shifts away laughing, he captures it, tucking it into his hip, secured with his elbow.

"Mostly. First, I don't snore," I say adamantly.

"You say that..."

"Two"—I draw the word out, getting us back on track—"I was actually talking about Jake. How do you so seamlessly correct that attitude and at the same time command respect?" I scoot down further on the couch and free my trapped foot, resting it on his thigh. "Do you have a bunch of nephews? Secret kiddos of your own hidden in every port?"

Miles's hands still briefly in their massage before he clears his throat and tilts his head to the side, cracking his neck. "I have four nieces. My younger sister," he adds when he sees my questioning look. "She married her high school sweetheart and lives near my parents' farm."

"How old are they?"

"The oldest is six, the twins are four, and the youngest just turned one."

My eyes widen. "Twins. Really? Jack and Kate's oldest are twin boys. I can't imagine."

Finally, the stress I saw twist his lips stretches into happiness. "They're Irish twins actually, eleven months apart, but they look a lot alike. All the girls do." And there's that sadness back again.

"You miss them?" I guess.

"I do." He goes back to rubbing my foot, digging his thumbs in, working my tension away as he battles his own. "I get back to Iowa to see them when I can."

"Does your family ever come to visit you? Oh, have they ever seen the ocean?"

I so take it for granted that everyone has experienced the power of the ocean, perfectly balanced with the calm serenity of it. Growing up in the Midwest, it's a distinct possibility that they haven't.

After a pause, Miles blows out a deep breath, almost forcing the tension to leave his shoulders. "They all came to California a couple of years ago, so everyone but the baby has. The middle two probably don't remember any of the trip." A shrug hitches at his shoulder, his movement stiff and uncomfortable.

I pull my foot from his hands, sit up, and push the coffee table away from the couch. "Come here." I pat the floor in front of me.

A laugh chuffs from Miles, a little reserved. "Why do I need to sit on the floor?" He folds his big body onto the floor and leans his back against the couch.

"Take off your shirt," I tell him, swinging my legs so they rest one on either side of him. And, Lord, when he does, muscles flex and ripple in a mouthwatering display.

He hums as I drag my nails through his thick, dark hair and down the back of his head.

He groans as I grab hold of his trapezius, and he rolls his shoulders back as I dig my thumbs into the tight muscles.

I knead and dig, pinch and push until, finally, Miles melts, relaxing into my thighs.

"What are you doing to me?" he mumbles, low and husky.

"Returning the favor," I say. I lean forward and graze the curve of his ear with my lips. Nipping at the lobe. Kissing his neck just behind it. "You're always rubbing my feet, my legs—taking care of me. I want to do the same for you."

His groan as I kiss my way down the strong column of his neck, across the top of his back, spurs me on.

There is nothing more powerful than the feeling of making the person you care about feel good. And this thing with Miles has turned into more—much more—than me just caring about him. I can see him as part of us, part of our family.

EIGHTEEN

Miles

The more time I spend with Chloe and Jake, the more time I want to spend with them. It's like I can't get enough.

Without any planning or discussion, we've fallen into a comfortable routine. On the afternoons that Jake's team has practice, I skate out of work early to pick him up from school. We grab a bite to eat, pick up Bronson, and head for the rugby pitch.

God knows, with as early as I've been getting into the office, I'm putting in almost a full workday by the time lunch rolls around.

Jason leans out of his office and stares intently until I can practically feel his thoughts running. "Miles, you got a minute?" It's not really a question when the owner of the company you work for asks it.

"Yep." I push back from my desk and stand, stretching out my back.

As I close my laptop, popping it off the docking station,

Jason taps the top of my desk with his keys and adds, "Let's go grab a bite to eat."

Erin's office door is closed, and any hope I have of getting a read from her on what this impromptu meeting is about is squashed. The glow of her monitors reflects off her computer glasses, hiding her eyes. She's hunched forward, concentrating, though I can't be sure if it's on whatever she's working on or if she's just focused on avoiding making eye contact.

I pull my keys and wallet from my drawer, tuck my phone into my pocket, and follow the big boss out into the clear spring day.

"What are you feeling like? New River Tap House?" Jason asks without looking up from his phone.

Normally, I wouldn't be fazed by the attention, the request for lunch, any of this, but with the way plans have been changing lately, I just don't know.

"Sure. Sounds good." I pause, waiting for a sign that he's heard me.

Seconds tick past, scrolling into minutes.

Finally, Jason raises his head and lifts his chin toward his vehicle. "How are things?" he asks bluntly.

"Good." I pull the seat belt across me, clicking it into place.

"Your performance at work is solid, man. I'm not questioning that. I want to know how you're doing outside of that. Personally. You and Chance still tight? Coaching rugby?"

I nod along at each thing he mentions.

"What about the other stuff?" he asks more solemnly.

I huff out a surprised laugh. "You getting touchy-feely on me here?" I slide my aviators off and toss him an eyebrow waggle.

"Not my type, though I can't blame you for hoping." He tosses a wink back at me.

A hint of relief pushes away some of the tension that sprang into my shoulders the minute I was summoned.

"The other stuff. You've been busting out early, and that trip to California was canned? What's happening there? Anything I need to know?"

I shift in my seat, the tension rolling back in, pulling my muscles tight. "I'm not skipping out. I've been getting in early, around five most mornings. If I need to adjust back to what I was doing before, I will. I didn't think it would be a problem."

Jason doesn't know Chloe, and his kids are too young to have her as a teacher, but he doesn't need to know why I'm up and out of bed at the ass crack of dawn every morning. Hell, I can't remember the last time I spent the night at my apartment.

"Flexible hours, man. You work when it suits you. I just want to make sure you're good. Not struggling with..." He glances at me before spinning the steering wheel and backing into a spot in the far corner of the lot.

"No, no. I'm good." I give him a brief outline on what the trip was for and why it was postponed.

While Calvin Feuerborn was right there while I was in California, going through my worst nightmare in real time, Jason has only gotten an overview. The highlights.

"Jesus Christ, you've got to be fucking kidding me," he says as we walk into the restaurant. Jason bypasses the hostess stand and walks straight to the bar, pulling out two barstools and planting his ass in one. "Pretty sure I'm going to need a beer after hearing that." He holds two fingers up and points to the tap with a local brew.

"We drinking on company time, boss?" The hoppy brew releases a tropical citrus burst as I take a cautious sip.

Jason, on the other hand, drains a third of his pint, turning to me as he sets the glass back down on the ratty paper coaster. He huffs out an uncomfortable laugh, pushing his blond hair back from his face. "I don't know whether to kick your ass or applaud you. How... how the hell are you so fucking good?" he asks incredulously.

I get it. What happened with my ex-wife isn't something I discuss often. Generally, I avoid talking about it at all costs, but as my boss, Jason needs to know. "I'm not. Not at all. I'm just trying to do the right thing. Make sure a tragedy ends the best way it can for everyone." I shrug and pull a menu toward me, studying every line of each description, hoping that we can drop the subject.

"You really are a goddamn mild-mannered superhero. How did you not lose your mind and go all Bizarro?"

In need of an escape, I nod to the bartender and place my lunch order. After she sashays down to the register at the other end of the bar, I roll my pint glass between my palms. "You don't know that I didn't. Talk to Calvin. He saw the shitshow. Had front row seats to it." I pick at the frayed edge of my coaster, making a small pile out of the bits of paper.

I can feel Jason wanting to say something more, something important. Some sage nugget of wisdom to soothe the chafing burn of the senselessness of a pointless loss. But there's not a damn thing he can say—that anyone can—that will make any difference. Much as I hate the saying, it is what it is.

"Miles—"

"You know, sometimes, I wonder if there was some higher lesson I was supposed to learn from the whole thing. Something that maybe I'd missed in a former life. An opportunity I missed in this one, and losing her—them—is my punishment." I steal a glance at him from the corner of my eye. "Like, somehow, I deserved it. Earned it."

"I can't believe that, man. No one deserves that kind of trauma." Jason drains his beer. Silently, he orders another round.

"I don't know. If I can't find the lesson, the least I can do is try to do right by the whole thing."

"Well, we're here for you, man. Anything you need."

"About that," I start, holding my breath.

Jason pins me with an arched brow. I'm almost certain he's already dreading his offer.

"I'm going to have to bounce when I get the call from Aly's lawyer. I'm guessing I won't have a ton of notice before I need to leave, so until then, is it cool if I keep working the odd hours? In early, out early? Hell, I don't really even need to leave early most days. I just... Whatever I can work ahead on is what I'm doing."

Jason nods, huffing out a laugh. "You don't have to kill yourself with the job. It'll be there when you get in and still fucking be there at the end of the day. I'm not worried about things falling through the cracks, not from you."

I wish I felt the same way. Instead, all I feel is the looming potential of disappointment.

"WHY ARE we digging up all the grass?" Jake asks. "Does this mean I won't get paid as much?" He leans against the fence at the back of the small lot, draping his arms along the length, sagging dramatically.

"Nope. Pay is for the job, not per blade of grass. Come on. Let's get the grass up before your mom decides to make her garden bigger." The spade cuts through the sod, lifting it in clumps.

Jake works, humming something that sounds a hell of a lot like one of the songs for his video game. Knocking dirt from the clods of grass and chucking them into the wheelbarrow.

By the time we are down to bare earth in some curved pattern that Chloe drew out for reference, Jake and I are hot, sweaty, dirty messes.

"You boys want a cold drink first, or should we go straight to the garden center to pick up dirt and plants?" Chloe asks, juggling a couple of big cups filled to the brim with ice and water and... *cucumber?*

Jesus, she put chunks of cucumber in the water.

I take a cup and sip, tasting. And then I drain it. The cold water, while good on its own, is better, more refreshing with the light flavor I can't even describe.

"It's good, right?" She's smiling huge, relaxed and happy.

"It is. Not used to drinking my salad unless it's in a protein shake or smoothie, but this is..."

"It's weird," Jake says, cutting in. "She always hides veggies —like, in everything. I *know* you do it with muffins and other stuff, Mom," he adds, plucking cukes from his water like they're bugs floating but popping them in his mouth anyway.

Chloe shrugs. "Yep. You've got me all figured out, don't you? Okay, are we ready?" She collects the empty cups and marches back across the yard, her sweet ass swaying, ponytail bobbing.

Dear God, she's beautiful.

"Let's go, bud," I say, wrapping a hand on Jake's shoulder, steering him after his mom.

"I just don't understand why we need any more dirt. She always does this stuff, and it's crazy." Jake rolls his eyes and throws his hands out, letting them fall to his sides.

"Yeah, this one falls under *work hard* and *respect your elders*. And when in doubt, just do what your mom says. That's probably the best rule to live by."

We pile into my truck and spend the next couple of hours picking out flowers and vegetables. Dirt and rocks and mulch. Chloe agonizes over decisions. Which colors to put together. Which variety of tomato plant. Carrots and cucumbers, beans and berries. And Jake and I just follow along behind her. Pushing the cart, checking out the flowers in other people's carts, looking at the pictures of full blooms on the little tags.

"What about this one?" I hand Chloe a plastic pot with a bunch of leaves and nothing else. I bite down on my lip to fight a smile as she scrunches up her face.

"What is that?" She takes the pot from me and looks at the tag. "Poppies?"

I glance over my shoulder. Jake is at the end of the row, looking at the Venus flytraps.

"Mmhmm. Those pretty pink petals remind me of—*oof.*"

The back of Chloe's hand whacks me in the stomach as her face turns the most beautiful shade of pink, deeper than the petals in question.

Yeah, she knows exactly what those delicate folds remind me of.

"Oh my God, I can't believe you." Her head darts around as she checks to see if anyone is paying any attention to us.

News flash: they weren't until she backhanded me.

"I like it. I think we need to get some."

"No."

"Why not? They're actually really pretty," I say, picking up two more pots.

She said something earlier about clusters of threes.

Chloe takes the poppy plants out of my hands and sets them back with the others. "Because you ruined it." She laughs. "I'll never be able to look at poppies again without thinking about..." She waves her hands around in the air, her cheeks getting redder.

She takes charge of our full cart and steers it away from the flowers I desperately want to get now, toward the front of the garden center, Jake and I falling into line behind her again.

"Oh, hang on. There's one more thing I need to grab. You guys get in line. I'll be right back." She ducks down an aisle and disappears from sight.

"Did you have a garden at your old house?" It's not often that I bring up their old house with Jake. They moved here to get on with life and leave the past behind.

"Yeah, but alls we had to do was plant new things and then pick them. My dad did all the hard stuff when I was little."

Jake was young when he lost his dad, probably doesn't have a ton of strong memories of him, but he doesn't shy away from talking about Dallas. I swear Chloe has a harder time with it than Jake.

Before long, we're at the front of the line, the cashier scanning each plastic pot with her gun, and finally, Chloe's black curls bob up the side of the line.

"What the hell?" I laugh. "Why didn't you let me lug the tree up here while you waited in line?"

She leans back, stopping her flatbed next to the one Jake and I babysat while Chloe was wrestling an entire tree onto her cart. "Did you already get the dirt and—"

"It's on there. We just need to swing around the back of the store and load it." I flip the tag from the tree for the cashier to scan and reach for my wallet.

"What are you doing? You're not paying for my garden." Chloe bats at my hand and reaches inside the top of her shirt.

I would totally pay for her garden—*our garden?* I definitely feel invested.

She pulls out a credit card, wiping it on her yoga pants. "What?" she asks. "I wiped it off, no boob sweat."

"Yeah, there's still boob sweat," I say, reaching for my wallet again. "We'll just use mine."

Chloe reaches past me and pumps a glob of hand sanitizer onto the tips of her fingers. With a dark brow cocked above the frame of her sunglasses, she rubs the gel onto her hands and then over the plastic card, wiping it on the bottom of her shirt this time.

"There. It's clean." She slides it into the slot of the card reader and signs on the kiosk. She smiles, takes the receipt, and wheels her cart out to the truck.

At least she allows me to hoist the ornamental cherry tree into the bed of the truck. "You know this thing isn't going to produce fruit, right? Nothing edible anyway."

Chloe blows at a stray curl that escaped from the mass on her head and unloads the other cart with Jake. "That's fine, Superman. I know. You do the heavy lifting, dig the hole, and let me have my dreams of my farm. There are things I miss from New York, and the orchard down the road is one of them. Don't you crush my dreams."

NINETEEN

Chloe

With dinner over, the dishes done, and Jake finally tucked away in bed for the night, I look for the finishing touches for my pretty garden.

"What do you think of this?" I spin my laptop, so Miles can see the handmade garden bench.

He leans across the couch, squinting. He scrolls through the pictures, stopping finally on the map showing where it's located. "It's lovely. You're not getting it." He sits straight and kicks his feet up on the coffee table, searching through the channel guide way too fast for a normal person to process what might be on.

I laugh. "What do you mean, I'm not getting it? It's perfect for that spot in the garden. It should fit in the back of my car, right?"

"I love that you teach math and have no sense of spatial awareness," he says on a chuckle. "No, babe. It's not going to fit in the back of your vehicle, and no, you're not going to go and get it. It's in a shit part of town."

"Well, let me use your truck."

His head doesn't even move, just his eyes slide to the side, pinning me with an incredulous look.

"Not Maggie. I wouldn't dream of asking you to share your baby with me. I can take the other one. It'll be fine," I say, focusing on the Messages app.

I ask the usual questions. *Is it still available? Will you take less? Is tomorrow a good time to pick it up?* Sure, I'm getting ahead of myself by listing all the questions at once, not waiting for a response. But it's perfect.

The screen of my laptop slowly lowers until I have to pull my hands from the keyboard. Miles takes it from me, placing it on the end table next to him, well out of my reach.

"Chloe, I have no problem with sharing with you. You want to drive Maggie? That's cool. I would love to see my girls together, bonding. Your delicate hands wrapped around her steering wheel. Watching you work her clutch and take her through her gears."

His molten chocolate eyes darken as he turns to put his back to the arm of the sofa. His t-shirt bunches as he shifts, revealing a sliver of his taut belly.

He reaches forward, hooking a hand around each of my knees and pulling toward him. "In fact, I think it'd be hot as fuck to see you perched on her hood. One of those skirts you wear to work, your blouse gaping open, legs crossed, and those fuck-me shoes you have. Jesus." Miles slides his hands down my legs and tucks my feet on either side of his hips.

Goose bumps pop up along my skin on the path he trails

with calloused fingers. "You want dirty teacher pictures of me, Miles?"

"Dirty teacher, naughty librarian, whatever you want to call it. I call it art—pinup, nose art. Fucking beautiful."

Desire pools low in my belly as he describes in intimate detail exactly which skirt and blouse, the specific pair of shoes, even adding the detail of stockings with seams running up the backs of my legs. "Sounds like you've given this a lot of thought. Actually, I'm pretty sure I was wearing almost that exact outfit the night we officially met at the Amarre's house."

Miles chuckles, nodding slowly. "Oh, I've given it all kinds of thought. Thought about it on an incredibly hard drive home that night." He reaches down to adjust his growing erection. "I stroked my dick to the thought of you laid out over Maggie's hood that night in the shower. Came pretty fucking hard." He pushes himself off the couch, settling his knee between my thighs. He crawls up, stretching out above me, his hips notched in tight. He supports his weight on his elbows, framing my face between his big, warm palms.

"Did you?" I ask, trailing my fingertips down the center of Miles's strong back, mapping the deep groove of his spine between ridges of tight muscle. "You did good work with your imagination. Pretty sure I wasn't wearing stockings that night, and I know for a fact I don't have any with seams."

He groans against my neck as my hands push beneath his shorts, pulling him in closer to me. Miles rocks his hips against me, rubbing against my aching clit, the friction delectable.

"Definitely need to remedy that. Get you some garters, too." His tongue darts out, trailing down my throat to dip into my collarbone.

In a blur of motion, I'm in his arms, and once again, Miles

takes the stairs, silently stealing down the hallway and into my room.

"SO, you really don't mind if I take her for a spa appointment?" It's not a lie, not really.

Puss 'n' Pits provides spa services, just not for Miles's truck. But after he shared his spank material with me, I found the business card Jasmine had slipped into my hand and called Jensen to see if he would take my picture.

Miles shoots me a look. "Why would I mind? I told you last week, I like the idea of you behind Maggie's wheel." He tosses me the keys and adds, "Jake and I have some errands to run today, so take your time."

I check my tote bag to make sure that I have everything I need. When I called Jasmine to tell her what Jensen and I had planned, she said not to worry about anything. But my makeup bag has all my favorites products.

"Okay, I guess I'll see you boys later, then. Have fun and make good choices," I say as I squeeze out the door.

I hook my hangers over my finger, the thin plastic film from the dry cleaner billowing out behind me as I slide into Miles's beloved truck before hurrying to Puss 'n' Pits.

"You're here," Jasmine screeches when I walk through the door. "Flip the sign and roll the lock closed, would you, darlin'? We are on a tight schedule." Her hips sway as she leads me back to her office.

Curling irons of various sizes line one side of the makeshift vanity counter. Makeup palettes, brushes, hair spray, and an array of other beauty products fill the other. I hang my clothes on the edge of the door and pull my makeup bag from my tote.

"This seems woefully inadequate," I say, placing the orange-fuchsia-and-white swirled bag next to Jasmine's assembled tools.

"I told you, you didn't need to bring anything. Have a seat here, sweetie. Let's get this party started." She spins the desk chair and pats it.

The minute my tush hits the chair, Jasmine works efficiently and furiously. Working my glossy raven hair, meticulously straightening it, only to set it in fat rollers. While those set, she gets to work on my face. Layers upon layers of foundation, concealer, contouring and highlighting. My eyes, dark and sultry, with mile-long lashes and perfectly winged lines. My lips stained blood red, a layer of matte lipstick over top for the finishing touch.

"Dear Jesus, you're gonna rev that man's engine. All right, let's get this hair going, and then we'll get you dressed." She gently pulls the curlers from my hair, brushing it into perfectly beachy waves, twisting the front back and pinning fat, round rolls back on each side. Blast after blast of hair spray fills the air and fixes my hair into 1940s vogue.

"Wow."

Jasmine rests her hands on my shoulders and gives me a little shake.

"Fucking wow is right," Jensen says, filling the doorway. His blond hair is buzzed close on the sides today, his Viking heritage showing strong. "You got the keys to that badass truck out there? I'll move it into the shade while you finish getting ready, so you don't burn your ass when you hop up on the hood."

"In my tote. Hand it to me and—"

"Got 'em." He dips his hand in and pulls the keys from the depths, dragging my ruby-red bra with it. Jensen smirks, his brow raised high as he carefully separates the delicate lace from the edge of the wire key ring. "He's a lucky man. I'll be outside when you're ready." He flips the keys around his finger and stalks out the door.

"My God, that man makes my blood burn through my veins." Jasmine leans back, gaze pinned to him until the locks auto-click shut. "Okay then. So, we're going with classy pinup? Did you just bring the one outfit, or are we doing a wardrobe change?"

I pull the rest of my lingerie from my bag and look around for a bathroom. "I just brought the one. Do you have a restroom?"

"Next door down. I'm going to run upstairs to my apartment and just grab a couple things."

I pop into the restroom and change. The red lace bra lifts my boobs and pushes them together, creating cleavage I never knew I could have. The panties and matching garter are next. The stockings though are a challenge.

When I purchased them, the saleslady made it look so easy to roll them on, getting the seam perfectly straight up the back of the leg. It takes me several tries and some minor adjustments before I give up. Close enough is close enough.

Navy pencil skirt, short-sleeved white blouse, and bright red pumps that perfectly match the lace of my bra. I step out of the restroom and tuck my tote back into Jasmine's office.

"You ready?" she asks.

"As ready as I'll ever be." My gaze washes over the pictures lining the hall outside Jasmine's treatment rooms. "I can't wait to see what mine look like."

"Jen's got a good eye. They're going to be unreal." Jasmine leads me outside to where Maggie sits at an angle in front of Jensen's shop.

"You mind if we get a few in front of the shop?" he asks. "The lighting is on point, and—fuck me..." His words trail off as he turns to fully take me in. "Hot damn, honey. Just... damn."

Jensen offers me his hand and helps me up onto the hood of the truck. Nerves skitter through my belly, and as he starts taking test shots and making adjustments, I realize it must show.

"Chloe, relax. You've got to stop grittin' your teeth, doll. You look angry."

I paste on a smile, and after a couple of clicks, he sets the camera in the bed of the truck and leans against the bumper, arms over his chest, legs crossed at his ankles. "Jaz said you're from New York."

I adjust the hand I'm leaning on and tilt my head, relaxing ever so slightly. "I am."

"And what brought you down here?"

So, the conversation starts. We talk about me and Jake, about being closer to my family. We talk about my job and then how he made the switch from professional photographer to tattoo artist to owning his own shop.

As I relax, he picks up the camera and starts shooting again. Softly cueing me on small adjustments. Where to look. Where to place my hand. Saying something goofy when he wants me to laugh, the click of the camera coming like rapid-fire as he moves around the truck, looking for just the right angle.

"You doin' okay? Need a drink of water or somethin'?" he asks, standing straight.

"I'm good. Are we done already?"

We haven't been out here very long, but Jensen and Jasmine have businesses to run. I'm sure I've already taken up way too much of their time.

"Not at all. But do you think you're ready for something a little more..." Jensen hesitates.

"Provocative," Jasmine finishes for him. "Still classy but just a little bit... more, you know? You'll be blown away, I promise."

I think about it for a minute, biting at my lower lip, and the camera clicks. Jensen approaches and turns the camera, so I can see what he captured. I look good. Sultry. Sexier than I ever dreamed possible.

"Okay." I nod. "Let's do it."

And over the next couple of hours, Jasmine poses me, and Jensen takes pictures. When we break, it's only for a quick drink of water and for Jasmine to push me back into her shop to change. The high-waisted navy shorts and white halter top somehow leave me feeling more exposed than a bathing suit, but when we go back out, we fall back into the same easy conversation.

Finally, Jensen lowers the camera, a broad smile stretching his bearded face wide. "Yeah," he says, nodding. "Let me dump these on my laptop, and we can do a little preview, let you see what I got."

I slide off the hood of the truck, suddenly exhausted. "Is it cool if I change back into real clothes?"

"Absolutely," he calls over his shoulder as he stalks into the shop, camera in hand, pulling the memory card from the slot.

Jasmine leads me inside her shop and up the stairs to her apartment. "Help yourself to the shower. Figure since this is a surprise for your guy, you don't want to show up back home, looking like nose art. Towels, shampoo, everything you need is right there. I'll grab the rest of your stuff from my office for you and then meet you next door at Jen's," she says, already heading back down the stairs.

After a quick shower, my face clean, hair twisted back into the mess of black curls on the top of my head, I stuff my things into my tote and wander into the tattoo shop.

The receptionist smirks at me and throws her thumb over her shoulder. "Jen's office is the last door on the left. Girl, you looked fuck-hot."

"Thanks," I say, taken aback.

But when I walk through the door of Jensen's office, all I see is an image of me looking like I never in my life could have imagined.

TWENTY

Miles

With Chloe finally out of the house, I look at Jake and ask, "You ready to roll?"

He reaches behind him and pulls his shoes from under the couch, shoving his feet into them. For a kid, he did a damn good job, locking down the nervous jitters and acting cool.

"Yep. Let's do this." He bounces off the floor and struts to the door, Chloe's keys in his hand.

"You driving?" I ask, pulling the door shut behind us.

Jake snorts, laughing way too hard over my comment. "No. *Geebus*, Miles."

He makes a wild toss with the keys, and I have to jump to snag them.

"I don't think your mom would be okay with that one either. Cursing doesn't make you cool, man." I click open the locks and slide the driver's seat back as far as it'll go before climbing in.

"Is that one of the rules?" The click of a seat belt sounds from the backseat.

"It is. Being a gentleman is important business. No matter what, those rules are ones to live by." I back Chloe's vehicle out, and in minutes, we've swapped it out for my truck. It's times like these that I'm glad I have both. Not just because Chloe decided to be sweet and get Maggie detailed, but dirty work and moving things calls for a truck that's not a classic with a pristine walnut bed.

"Didn't you tell Mom it was too dangerous to go get this thing?" Jake asks, checking the lock on his door.

I chuckle and adjust my aviators. "I did."

"But it's okay for us to be here?" He looks around the slightly run-down neighborhood scrolling past us. "Because we're men and she's a girl?"

Tilting my head back and forth, I search for the right words. Talking to Chloe's son, teaching him the things he needs to know to be a true gentleman, has become important to me. I don't want to fuck it up. "We're going to call it being chivalrous. Taking care of the people we love, being honorable and protective." I turn down a street to the right and stop in front of a house halfway down the block.

"And that's one of the rules, too?"

"Yep. You're learning, kiddo," I tell him. We hop out of the truck and approach the older gentleman standing in the shade of the open garage door. "Stick right with me. I'm going to need your muscles to help move this thing."

I thrust my hand forward in greeting, Jake following suit. "This it?" I ask.

"It is," the gentleman replies. "Good you brought help; it

weighs more'n a bit. Had to have my son come by and bring it up here for you from the backyard."

I reach into my pocket and pull out the bills for the price we settled on. I didn't lowball the guy, but meeting him, seeing that he's an older man in a neighborhood past its prime, I almost wish I had agreed to the full asking price. "You made this?"

He accepts the money I hand him, pocketing it right away. "I did. The wife wanted a place to sit in her garden to read. What the wife wants, the wife gets." He chuckles, but there's a sadness behind it. "Made this and a little table to match. She'd sit out there for hours, reading her love stories, with a glass of tea. Now, she's in a home. Can't use it, so I'm glad your missus'll give it a good home."

That right there is some old-school love and devotion. "You looking to unload that table, too?" I ask.

"They sure do look pretty together. You think your lady might like it?" He rubs a handkerchief across his brow and stuffs it back in his pocket.

"I think she'd love it."

He names a price, and I hand him the cash without batting an eye. Jake and I get the bench and matching table loaded in the back of the truck and say our good-byes.

"That was really nice of you, buying that table, too," Jake says, clicking his belt.

"I think your mom'll like it, don't you?"

"She'll love it." He shifts in his seat, looking at me and then looking back out the windshield. "Thanks, Miles. This is going to be the best Mother's Day ever."

I nod and tousle his hair. My throat clogs, not letting even the simplest response through. That thank-you, this errand, might mean more to me than it does to him. It's nothing for me to help Jake get his mom something she wants for Mother's Day but spending time with them like this is huge. Fucking huge.

We stop to pick up a planter and dirt and a tray of poppies I ordered to set in the garden.

Our errands done, I look to Jake and say, "How about we stop at the convenience store and get a drink and a snack?"

His face lights up, and he nods furiously. He's such a good kid.

"All right then." I swing into the same convenience store where we first ran into each other. Where Chloe literally fell into my arms. And thank God for that.

I'm not at all surprised when Jake grabs the biggest cup and fills it to the brim. I pay and with a hand to his back guide him out to the truck. We climb in, and as I roll the windows down to let the heat out, a kid in his late teens flies out the doors, a purse grasped in his hand—one that looks a hell of a lot like the one the lady behind us in line had.

Shouts for him to stop and calls for help kick me into motion.

I jump out and lock the doors behind me. "Stay here, Jake. Don't leave the truck. I'll be right back."

I take off after the kid and see him just as he rounds the corner at the next block. Legs pounding, I eat up pavement between us, and it's not long before the kid tires and slows. I push myself harder, closing the gap.

Sirens wail, the sound getting louder as the police approach. When the kid glances over his shoulder, he stumbles before gaining his footing, but that little stutter-step is all I need. I'm close enough to turn up my speed, wrap him up, and take him to the ground.

In full panic, he tosses the woman's purse and tries to push me off. I've got easily six inches and fifty pounds on the kid. Training kicks in, and by the time the police car pulls up next to us, he's given up the fight.

Running through the details takes time. It should be completely obvious by the fear on the kid's face and the way he's practically shitting his pants that he's the one who grabbed the purse and ran, but the police have a procedure they have to follow. And then I have to get myself back to Jake. I jog it, impressed with just how far I chased the kid down.

The two police cars parked at the convenience store don't surprise me in the least as I round the corner. But the cop standing next to my truck, talking to Jake and the woman whose purse was grabbed, kick my pace up a notch.

"There he is," Jake yells, pointing toward me. "His code name is Superman." He unlocks his door, triggering the alarm.

I dig my keys from my pocket and hit the button to silence it as quickly as I can.

Jake jumps out and meets me at the front of the truck, beaming with pride.

"You're the one who took off after him?" the lady asks, stepping forward.

"I am," I manage while catching my breath. "The officers took your bag to the station with the kid." I look from her to the officer standing with her.

"Thank you so much. I don't know what I would have done. It was just such a surprise. That boy came out of nowhere. He was just so fast," she rambles. "I'd like to thank you properly, but my wallet, my cash—"

"No, ma'am. Not necessary. I was happy to help and glad that it all turned out okay."

She lunges forward and surprises me with a quick hug. "Thank you."

The officer directs her to the police station to start the process of claiming her purse. "I'll be there shortly to follow up," he adds before turning to me. "Not every man would abandon his son to chase down a criminal. Could have ended differently if that kid had a gun on him or if people were waiting for him around the corner." He rests his hands on his utility belt, his stance wide. There's a definite hint of lecture or maybe judgment in his tone.

"Yes, Officer. It was a calculated risk, but I trust this guy to make good decisions." I wrap my arm around Jake's back and give his shoulder a squeeze, hoping that he doesn't pick now to correct the cop, saying that I'm not his dad.

The cop nods, working his jaw back and forth. "Thanks, but maybe next time, just let us take care of things like this. You concentrate on taking care of your family, all right? Take care, buddy." He pats Jake on the back and climbs into his vehicle.

Jake and I get in the truck and take off toward home. Ice rattles in his cup, the sound clearly indicating his beverage is gone.

"You drink all of that already?" I ask.

He squirms in his seat and furiously nods his head.

"You gonna make it home, or do I need to gun it?" I glance at him and give the accelerator a little extra gas, just in case.

"I'm good," he answers. But the minute we pull into the driveway, Jake is out of the truck and running for the keypad on the garage door.

I unload the back of the truck, setting the table and planting crap to the side. The bench I hoist out and carry to the far back corner of the yard. I place it under the cherry tree

Chloe insisted on and angle it so that, hopefully, at least a small portion of it will sit in the shade.

I turn my head at the sound of a small grunt to find Jake lugging the full bag of potting soil across the yard.

"Didn't want to grab something a little lighter?" I ask.

"I can do it," he says, heaving the bag to the ground, narrowly missing a mound of flowers Chloe planted last weekend. He lunges, catching the bag at the last second and flopping it in the other direction.

"Nice save. Let's go haul the rest of the stuff and let Bronson out while we make this pretty for Mom."

It doesn't take all that long to move the side table back or plant the flowers in the pot. The lady at the garden store had me take a picture of what the finished product was supposed to look like, so when all is said and done, it looks slightly better than a hack job slapped together by an unsupervised bachelor and a kid.

"Hey, that looks kinda nice," Jake says with authority, his hands propped on his hips. "We make a good team."

"That we do." I glance at my watch. Several hours have passed since Chloe left this morning. "Your mom should be home soon. Let's go swap out cars real quick."

I gather up the trash from our planting project and head around the front of the house to see Chloe stepping out of the driver's side of Maggie, her huge tote bag hanging from her shoulder.

"Hey. That took some time. I didn't realize she was that dirty."

My gaze wanders over Chloe, noting that, while she looks fresh, her hair damp and face scrubbed clean of any makeup, the car she took for detailing doesn't look any shinier than it did before she left. The muscle in my jaw pops as I work through how to ask where the hell she's been all day. I pull my shoulders back and blow out a breath, preparing to ask, when Chloe sighs.

"Shit. I can't do this."

My heart stops, dread filling me. With my sunglasses in place, I have the advantage of cataloging her body language, picking apart each shift and movement to try and determine the depth of her deception.

"I don't want to lie, but I can't tell you everything. I didn't get your truck detailed today. I thought I'd have time, but I didn't. I'm sorry—"

"No apologies. We're not starting that shit up again. Where were you, Chloe?" I demand.

"Out," she says, squaring herself in front of me. Whatever nerves she was toying with a minute ago are replaced with a confidence that I'd find sexy as shit if I wasn't wondering what she had been doing and who she had been with that she needed to shower before coming home. "It's a surprise, something special I wanted to do for you, but I can't tell you about it yet. I need a couple weeks."

"And you needed my truck for this?" I question, brows arched.

She pushes past me, heading for the house. "I did."

I follow her through the garage and into the house. "Secrets don't make friends," I say.

Chloe stops and drops her bag to the floor. The clothes inside it shift to the side, giving me a glimpse of her fuck-hot bright red shoes, the white blouse, a neatly folded dark blue something that could very well be the skirt that perfectly molds to her ass—exactly the outfit I told her I'd jacked off to after dinner at Blake and Erin's.

I can't stop the smirk from spreading across my face. I don't do anything to stop myself as I prowl across the room to her. I cup her face in my hands and kiss her hard and deep, swiping my tongue across the seam of her lips, demanding entrance. Devouring her. I hold her against me, reveling in the feel of her, in the way we're connected. Her breasts smash against me, and our hips press into each other, my thigh wedged between her legs, tight against her core.

When Chloe is good and breathless, I murmur against her lips, "You're fucking perfect."

TWENTY-ONE

Chloe

Jake bursts through the back door, Bronson trotting along behind him, and I jump back from Miles. I don't have any illusions that Jake is completely clueless that something's going on with Miles and me. I'm just not ready for him to walk in on anything, and that kiss was quickly turning into something more than anything.

"Mom, did Miles tell you our secret?" Excitement shines in his eyes as he takes in what is obviously an embrace.

My concern over how Jake might react to seeing me with someone other than his dad skitters away. I slide my hands from Miles's sides, where I was pulling him to me, to his grooved abs where I'm playfully pushing him away. "Secret? Someone once told me that those don't make friends."

Miles lets out an *oof*, taking a step back and wrapping his arms loosely around his middle. It's apparent to all of us that he's faking the effects of being shoved. Hopefully, Jake misses the adjustment Miles makes to his erection, which was just pressed *hard* against me.

"Good thing we don't have to worry about that," he mutters through a smirk.

Jake cocks his head like a puppy. "Wait, I don't get it. Aren't you guys friends? Does that mean... What about the secret?" he asks.

"What secret, Jake? Go ahead and tell me."

I reach into the fridge and pull out ingredients for dinner. Baby potatoes, fresh green beans, and a pork tenderloin coated in cracked black pepper. While I wash the potatoes and prep them to roast, Jake looks to Miles, his brows arched high, a silent conversation marked with wild, exaggerated facial expressions and flailing hands. And when I glance over my shoulder at Miles, I'm relieved to see he looks as clueless as I feel.

"Jake, just spill it already. It's not like we're going to be able to hide it from her until Mother's Day." A deep belly laugh tumbles from Miles.

"Okay, so, Mom, listen to this, just listen. *Oh my glorb*, it was so flipping crazy." Jake jumps into his story, and now, it's Miles's turn to tilt his head from side to side, trying to figure out where this story is going. "So, we went and picked up that bench you wanted, so we could surprise you for Mother's Day because you're the best mom in the entire world—I'm not even joking. And—"

"Wait, you guys went to that neighborhood that you said was sketchy—too sketchy for me to go to?" I glare at Miles, who shrugs almost apologetically.

Jake continues. "Yeah, but that's 'cause we're the men and being chiva..."

"Chivalrous," Miles finishes for him.

"Right, chivalrous. That's it. We were being chivalrous, and that's one of the rules, so it's okay. So, we got it and the extra table that the guy had, too. And then we stopped and got flowers and dirt and stuff. And then, Miles said we could go get a drink from the fainting store, and—"

"Really?" I ask. "That's what we're calling it?"

"It fits." Miles grins, nodding toward the back door. "We should show your mom how nice it looks."

"Yeah, sure. But then, when we were leaving and getting in the truck, this kid runs out of the store with a lady's bag—her, um... her..."

"Purse?" I tense, my knuckles turning white around the handle of my knife. I don't like where this story is headed.

"Yeah, her purse. And so, people run out, yelling, and Miles jumps out of the truck and takes off running after the guy. And Miles is fast, Mom—like, really fast."

Jake's gesturing wildly, and I've already lost count of how many times he's said *like, and,* and *so,* but I'm not at all excited with the direction this story is taking.

"And I stayed in the truck, just like Miles told me to. I stayed there, and I stuck my head out and talked to the lady. Told her that Miles would get her stuff back 'cause he's like a hero and stuff. And—"

"You... wait... you..." I can't even begin to wrap my head around the fact that my child was not just at a convenience store without me—something I have been adamant about not happening *ever*—but he was also there during a robbery.

"And then police cars came, and one went flying past—like, really fast. And the other one pulled in, and he—that cop— talked to the lady and the store manager and then, and then, and then he came over to Miles's truck and waited with me and the lady, and we all waited until Miles came running back. And the police guy, he said…"

As my eyes slam shut, I raise my hand, palm out, wanting nothing more than to stop everything—the words, the story, the worst of my fears playing out in a nightmare come to life. My heart races, my breaths come in shallow pants, and though I'm home, and I know we're all safe, the wave of panic pulls at me. I open my eyes, needing to orient myself.

One. Deep breath in.

Two. Hold it.

Three…

My vision tunnels, blackness closing in on me at an alarming rate, and I feel the floor slipping away beneath me.

A faint echo of, "Goddamn it. Stay with—"

And then it all goes blank.

"ALL RIGHT, son, wring it out good and hand it to me. Perfect."

Cold water hits the back of my neck, clinging to me in a way that doesn't make sense. Seconds tick by but everything feels like it's moving in slow motion until my eyelids crease and finally crack open.

"There she is." Miles's voice is deep but calm, wrapping around me in a soothing cocoon of soft, cool velvet. "Jake, hand me a bottle of water."

"Is this my fault? I didn't mean to…"

The sound of sorry-filled guilt, trepidation oozing out of Jake jolts through me like a slap across the face, throwing me into mama-bear mode. I sit up, pushing against the support holding me upright.

"Stop." I push hard, earning a loud *oof* from behind me as I launch my ass up off the kitchen floor, a cold, damp cloth falling away from my neck. Chills race down my spine as my blood boils in my veins.

"Chloe, take it easy," Miles says.

"Don't." I scramble to get my feet under me, wobbling slightly with the sudden movement.

In a flash, Miles is on his feet next to me, steadying me. "Careful, babe. Calm—"

"No. Just no." I shove his hands away. "Don't you tell me to calm down. Don't you fucking dare."

Jake gasps, saying, "Mom," at the same time Miles's chin jolts back, surprise battling with concern.

He reaches out again, but I push away, feeling like a trapped animal, scared and cornered.

"What made you think that was okay? That you could endanger my child like that?" My voice sounds foreign to me, high-pitched and shaky. A part of me knows that I'm overreacting. Not a lot, but enough. I should calm down—at least for Jake's sake—but I can't. I just can't.

"Chloe, please. He was safe. I would never—"

"You don't know that," I scream.

Miles turns to look over his shoulder. "Jake, go on upstairs for a minute, okay? Let's give your mom some space. I promise, I'll be up in a just a little bit."

"Yes, sir," Jake says, tears in his eyes, feet pounding up the stairs.

Miles turns back to me, hands resting on his hips, and he

just waits… though not for long. The moment I hear Jake's bedroom door slam closed, I let loose my fears.

"Do you not get it? Do you just not get the significance? My husband—Jake's father—died in a robbery just like that. In a convenience store, just like that. Kids fucking around, stealing shit, and Dallas died. He had been trained, same as you. Fought. Pulled multiple tours, and he fucking died, Miles. He died. Do you have any idea what that feels like?

"And you took the last of him—the last remaining bit of my husband—my innocent child, and you knowingly left him in a situation that was already dangerous. You left him *alone*. How could you for a minute think that was okay? How can you stand there and spout shit about not keeping secrets when you didn't even have the balls to tell me what had happened today?"

My heart pounds against my ribs, and blood rushes hot through my veins. Black spots pop up in front of me, and I feel my vision clouding, tunneling again.

"Breathe in, two, three, four. Hold. Out, two, three, four." Miles walks me through the exercise, counting for me as I try to calm down.

I close my eyes and allow it, doing all I can not to pass out again. I'm all Jake has. I have to keep my shit together and protect him, keep him safe.

"What do you think I was doing, Chloe? Jake was safe. Completely safe. The windows were down, the vehicle was locked, and I had the fob. If he unlocked that door, the alarm would have sounded. I would never put Jake or you in harm's way. Not ever," he says as if responding to what I thought were strictly my thoughts. "Yes, you totally said all of that out loud. But you're not alone, Chloe, not in this."

I want to melt into his words, wrap myself up in the promise he made. Cocoon myself in a life that includes Miles.

"I'm here. I'm with you guys, one hundred percent." He closes the distance between us, his big palms warm against my cheeks as he gently cups my face. "There is no place in the world I'd rather be, no one I'd rather be with. You and Jake are all I need."

Deep chocolate eyes, flecked with hints of gold, scan my face, searching, waiting. The smallest tug of pressure against the back of my skull guides me closer to Miles.

"I'm sorry," he says.

"I can't lose him, Miles."

"I know. I won't jeopardize that. I won't risk it."

"He's my world." I beg him to understand, to truly understand the devastation that losing my child would cause me.

"Please," he pleads, so much pain and yearning overflowing in that one word. "Please believe me. Give me another chance. Forgive me. I don't want to lose either of you." His lips hover just above mine. "Please." A breath away.

I nod, the movement barely perceptible but enough that Miles skates his lips over mine. Kissing me softly. Gently. Need pushes us together, but fear of loss, of smothering this flame, holds me back from completely letting go.

"Miles," I whisper against his lips, "no more secrets. None, not ever."

Is it fair of me to demand this? I don't honestly know. We all have secrets, little ones. Gifts, surprise dinners, happy things. But not the big stuff. There's no room for secrets in the life-and-death things.

The shift is small, and I can't really decide if it's a shift toward me or away. Maybe it's just a settling acceptance, but when Miles pulls back from me, I feel lost in a way I hate down to my very soul.

"There are things I can't share, not until they're done. I have a trip to California coming up. I don't know exactly when or how long I'll be gone, but I have to go. There are things I have to take care of." His gaze darts back and forth between my eyes, searching, begging. Pleading for me to understand.

I suck a deep breath in and slowly push it out. "Work." I don't even bother to pose it as a question because I know, without a doubt, that there are things he absolutely can't tell me. Details I can't know. There's a level of trust that's required for being with a man like Miles, like Dallas, or any one of these men who put their lives on the line for us. Who live dangerously so that we can live free.

"As long as we have honesty at home, no secrets between us."

Miles answers me with a kiss, so deep, so full of desire that everything else is forgiven.

TWENTY-TWO

Miles

"Why are you doing this to yourself? Do you... do you still love her?" Erin asks the question I've been asking myself for years.

And finally, I have the answer.

"Aly?"

"Yeah."

"I will always love her; she was my wife. She gave me the most beautiful gift I could have ever imagined. But it's over between us."

"So, you're not hoping to be with her again? Restart your life together when she's better, get remarried when she gets out?"

I don't know how I got so lucky to have Erin as my friend. I adore my sister, but Erin is like the big sister I didn't have. She doesn't hold back. Doesn't take sides. Doesn't shy away from difficult discussions.

"No, Erin. Aly's not going to get better. And I can't. There's no way I can ever forget what she did. I will never be able to look at her and not see the bloody knife clutched in her hand. I will never not see my daughter's lifeless body lying in her bassinet. I can forgive Aly in a way because of how sick she was—*is*. I missed the signs—"

Erin cuts me off midsentence. "So did the doctors."

Ryan's said the same thing to me. Not just once. He says it every time we talk. Every single time.

"I know. But as sad—as *mad* as I am, I own that I could've done more. I should have. And while I'm willing to entertain forgiveness, I can't forget. And I can't see her anymore. The best I can do is make sure she's taken care of and that she has access to the help she needs and isn't just locked up with murderers and drug addicts. Deliberation didn't take long, and sentencing was even faster. I'm glad she's in an institution—her new place should be a good fit for her—but I have to walk away. This was good-bye. One hundred percent good-bye."

My long stride eats up the distance between security and my gate. I'm seven hours away from my future. A flight away from a family that I feel like I'm a part of.

Chloe and Jake are perfect, solid. I'm not afraid of hard work, dirty diapers, or sleepless nights. I'm not afraid of babies or kids, tweens or teenagers. Parenting doesn't scare me any more than the next guy just because of what I've gone through. I think it's life's greatest adventure, and I want to climb on to that roller coaster and live it with them.

"Erin, my flight's boarding. I've got to let you go. Just... don't expect me to come into work tomorrow. I have something I have to do." There's no doubt in my mind that she can hear the smile in my voice. The stress and strain melting off of my shoulders.

"I'll see you in a couple of days. Fly safe." She ends the call.

For the first time in two years, I feel good. Really, honestly good.

I jog the last few yards to the gate, and the attendant smiles broadly as I step up and scan my boarding pass.

"Enjoy your flight, Mr. Kent."

I thank her and walk down the jetway, pulling the strap of my bag over my head, a line of wrinkles creasing my shirt across my chest.

My flight is not at all full, and a little over halfway back, there's a completely empty row. Not a soul on either side of the aisle and plenty of space overhead for my bag. I pull my noise-canceling headphones free, stow the bag above my seat, and settle in by the window.

While I still have a hot minute, I tap out a text to Chloe. I doubt she's available, but I want her to know I'm thinking of her.

> Miles: I'll be home tonight.

I fasten my seat belt and slide my big headphones over my ears, the sounds of the announcements fading away to nothing. I scroll through my playlist, selecting one that I use for relaxation, meditation, whatever it's called. I'm about to switch to Airplane mode when a reply pops up on my screen.

> Chloe: I can't wait to see you.

A stupid big smile stretches across my face. I type out a quick *I love you*, and my thumb hovers over the Send button. *Should I? Should I wait?*

The flight attendant stops in the aisle next to my row.

I pull back one side of my headphones, so I don't speak too loudly. "Got it. Airplane mode." I tap the icon on the screen and turn it for her to see.

And then I close my eyes, allowing the peaceful feeling of a job well done, my task complete, to wash over me. The plane propels forward down the runway, pushing me deep into my seat, and California drops away.

THE QUIET SHIFT and collective waking of the passengers on the plane pull me out of the sleep of the dead.

"Sir, we're on our final approach to Norfolk. I need you to face forward and fasten your seat belt, please," the attendant says softly.

With slow, stiff movements, I drag my leg off the seat next to me and turn myself in the seat. My knees are wedged into the back of the seat in front of me, my clothes are a wrinkled mess, and I want a toothbrush more than anything. But I feel amazing. On top of the world. Finally at peace.

I stretch my arms over my head, vertebrae shifting and popping. The only tension sitting in my neck and shoulders is from sleeping in a funky position, and even that's not bad. On missions, I caught Zs in less comfortable places for sure.

The attendant comes through the cabin again, her bag out, collecting trash. I slept through the entire flight. A full seven hours.

The only other time that happens is when I'm wrapped around Chloe, her tucked into my chest and my arm locked securely around her waist. There's no soft, sleepy wake-up though. She tends to jump from the bed, panicked and throwing clothes at me as she pulls on whatever she's got close. Then, she ushers me down the hall, still trying to keep our sleepovers from Jake.

I wanted to laugh the first time she shoved me into the guest room across the hall from Jake's room, intent on hiding the fact that I'd spent the night. Even bleary-eyed with sleep, stumbling to the bathroom, Jake noticed me and that the guest bed hadn't been slept in. He even backed up a couple steps and rubbed his eyes, taking in the perfectly placed mountain of throw pillows.

The kid is way smarter than Chloe wants to admit. Knew all the mechanics of sex when I finally bit the bullet and took him out to have *the talk*. Someone had to make sure he knew what was going on, and Chloe flat-out told me she was ostriching hard on that one—head in the sand in full avoidance mode.

But he knew. Knew about girls and sure as hell knew that I hadn't crawled sleepily into the guest room after staying up late to finish a movie, like Chloe had told him. Her stuttering and nerves alone would have clued him in if he needed the extra push.

The whine of the engines shifts, the captain mumbles his unintelligible spiel through the speakers, and then the tires squeal against the tarmac.

I'm home.

My mind races with all the things I want to say, all the things I want to do. I slide to the aisle seat, headphones in hand, my thumb tapping against the hard plastic. As soon as the plane is at the gate, I'm up and out of my seat snagging my bag. Headphones tucked away, I throw the strap of my duffel across my chest and wrap an arm around it, holding it close.

I nod to the attendants, thank the captain, and hit the ground, moving out with a purpose. It's on the shuttle halfway to long-term parking before I remember to take my phone off Airplane mode. I bounce the black plastic case against my thigh, debating on giving Chloe a heads-up on my plans for her tonight, to see if I need to pick anything up on my way over.

Still weighing the pros and cons, I step out of the shuttle and make the short walk to my truck—not Maggie. She's not one I'd leave unattended in the airport parking lot for a week. I throw my bag in the backseat and climb behind the wheel, rolling the windows down to let the cool night air in. My phone connects to Bluetooth and immediately rings with a call.

"Ryan? What's going on?" I pull through the toll lane and swipe my card to pay for parking.

In no way could I ever suspect, let alone prepare for, what's about to hit me.

"Miles, I don't know how to tell you this. There aren't words to express how sorry—"

Training takes over, pushing emotion aside, and I steer my vehicle to the shoulder and hit the hazard lights. Whatever Ryan needs to tell me, I need to focus. "What happened?" I demand, voice steady and low.

Ryan hesitates and stutters, something I've never heard the man do in all the time I've known him. "Aly... The staff, they..."

"Ryan, spit it out. Tell me what happened."

I glance at the clock on my dash, the numbers glowing against the faded light of streetlamps filtering into the cab. It's about dinnertime in California. Aly should be settling in at her new long-term-care facility. I'm sure the stress of the past week, the disruption to her routine, the change in her environment have been difficult for her.

"She's gone. The staff went into her room to get her for dinner, and she was unresponsive. She—"

My heart slams in my chest. "She what?"

"She took her life," he says, the words barely audible above the rushing of blood through my ears.

"You've got to be fucking kidding me," I yell. "How? How the fuck does a gravely ill, fragile fucking person on suicide watch complete that fucking task?"

"She left a letter for you."

"Fuck that, I don't want it."

"Hold on," Ryan says, the sounds of papers shifting and the squeak of an office chair filter through the phone.

"After everything I did, everything we worked for to keep her safe, out of prison, to get her the help she needed, she fucking killed herself. She fucking... What? Took the easy way out?" Nothing about this is easy.

He forges ahead, reading her final words to me, "'*I'm so sorry. Not being in my right mind at the time is no excuse for what I did. I took the life we created. Killed our baby. I can't live with myself. I can't live with what I did to us. Please, Miles, if you ever loved me, let me go. Just let me go.*'"

"Ryan—"

"She was sick, Miles. Her judgment was so warped that there was no sense of reality. So broken that she couldn't process right from wrong, didn't get the consequences of her actions."

"That's why I fought so hard. That's why I did everything I could to absolutely do right by her, to make sure she was safe, that she got treatment instead of just being locked away for the rest of her life—or worse, released back into the world where she could hurt someone again. And, I still failed. Not even my best was good enough."

"I assure you, there will be a full investigation into this. We will find where the breakdown was, and the responsible person will be held accountable." Conviction rings through Ryan's words.

His speech is lovely. Heartfelt and award-winning. But the fact is, it doesn't even matter.

What was it I said to Jason about this? That I thought there was some lesson I was supposed to learn from this? I don't see a lesson. There is nothing to indicate that education, advancement, understanding, or adaptation is happening in any way from this shit.

The only thing getting hammered into me—yet again—is that I don't deserve the privilege of caring for others.

My heart burst with pride the day I held my daughter in my arms, thrilled that she had come a little early, as eager to meet me as I was to meet her before my team's next mission launched.

My heart seized when the coppery scent of blood slapped me into a new reality as I stepped through the door to find Aly catatonic, clutching a bloody butcher knife.

My heart was ripped to shreds when, at the end of the blood trail, I saw my baby girl, lifeless in her bassinet.

Now, all that's left is anger.

"I've got to go, Ryan. Thank you for everything you've done to try and help. I appreciate it. I'm sure Aly's family appreciates it."

"I'll let you know what they uncover. Miles, I'm so sorry." And he is. It's evident, but I just can't do this anymore.

"Thanks. I'll talk to you later." I put my truck in gear and slam on the gas, throwing my phone across the cab. It sails through the open window, bouncing before the wheels of a semi send it to its grave.

I drive straight to my apartment. Leaving my bag in the truck, I go inside. It's dark, and the air is stale. I don't bother with any lights. I go directly to my liquor cabinet and turn a full bottle of whiskey upright. The burn is a welcome punishment as I swallow down gulp after gulp.

By the time the whiskey is nothing but a dribble of backwash in the bottom of the bottle, my heart is finally numb.

TWENTY-THREE

Chloe

Sunlight slashes bright across my eyes. But it's the tongue on my neck that really pulls me from sleep. Unfortunately, the tongue is attached to seventy pounds of hunting dog instead of the man I fell asleep waiting for. I lift one hand, shielding my eyes until I can adjust to the light intrusion, and wrap the other around Bronson's head. Sometimes, it's easier to stop the assault by pulling him in closer than by pushing him away.

The scrape of a spoon against a bowl and the slurp of milk are clear indicators that I'm not alone.

"Why'd you sleep on the couch?" Jake asks around a mouthful of cereal.

"Why are you sitting in the cozy chair with a bowl full of milk about to spill?" I push myself up to sitting and rub the sleep from my eyes. Sure that I'm sporting a stellar smudge of mascara, I pull the collar of my shirt up and swipe underneath. Lord, I feel like I got hit with a freight train.

I check the time on my phone and see there's nothing from

Miles. Not a message. Not a missed call. Nothing. What I do see is that my alarm didn't go off, and if I don't get my ass in gear, I'm going to be late for work.

"When you're done, make sure you rinse out your bowl and put it in the dishwasher."

I drag myself upstairs, tying my hair back as I go, and take a quick shower. It helps but not nearly enough. After a swipe of makeup with sound appreciation for the fact that curly hair can make for the cutest updo without a whole lot of effort, I dress casual and comfy. Perfect for a Friday and an end-of-section review day at school.

"Did you feed the dog?" I ask as I hop off the stairs and round the corner.

Jake is standing at the back door, dressed for school, his backpack on the kitchen table and a cup of coffee ready for me in my favorite to-go cup. "Yep. And he pooped."

Bronson proudly trots back in and goes straight to the end of the couch, where he spends the bulk of his day while we're gone.

"Thanks."

I'm in awe. Jake is such a different kid from the one who fought the move down here. Not different so much as better. Back to the one I knew was in there.

"I didn't know what you wanted for breakfast, so I just made you coffee," he says, his brows lowered in concern. "Does it taste right?"

Expecting a foul version of coffee, I gingerly take a sip. And another. I'm nothing short of pleasantly surprised. "It's perfect. When did you learn to make coffee?" I ask, pulling a protein bar from the pantry and dropping it in my bag for later.

"Miles showed me. He said it was part of the rules of manliness—to know how to make a good cup of coffee." Without another word, Jake checks the lock on the back door and throws his backpack over his shoulder.

And when he walks to the door, holding it open for me to pass through first, I have to admit, I. Am. Shook.

Bits and pieces of this elusive list have been discussed in my presence, but I'm sure I don't know nearly enough about it.

We climb into the car, and I set off to drop Jake off at school.

On the way to Cox High, I call Miles. His voice mail picks up immediately. "Hey, I crashed on the couch last night. Hope I didn't miss you. I kind of thought you were coming straight over from the airport. I'm pulling into school, so I'll talk to you later." I hesitate, catching myself before *love you* trips off my tongue. "Bye."

Maybe I should be shocked by the realization that the thought was so natural. That the feeling of loving Miles doesn't scare me the way I thought it would. I didn't expect it to happen again. I thought Dallas was my one and only, that love like that didn't happen twice in a lifetime. Once was a privilege. Twice is a damn gift.

EACH TIME I TEXT MILES, my phone shows the message as Sent, never switching to Read or even Delivered. I'm sure he's drained after from whatever dragged him to California. He was dreading the trip.

To get out faster at the end of the day, I have my last class flip chairs and clean the whiteboards, so we can all bolt for freedom together when the bell rings. I should have taken my time. The line of cars waiting to get out of the school parking lot is ridiculous.

Music blares, and brakes squeal as more than one car has to stop short because somebody wasn't paying attention the way they needed to. I should probably be scared, surrounded by new drivers who are more eager to leave school and start their weekend than usual. The semester is winding down, and the sun is shining. It's a perfect day to be young and dumb.

Except it's not. Worry niggles at the back of my brain. I just don't understand where Miles is. If his flight had been delayed, he would've called. Even if he had gotten tied up in a meeting, he would've sent a quick message. This complete and utter lack of anything isn't like him.

I bypass the turn for Jake's school and go straight to Miles's apartment. Both of his trucks are there, but as I park next to Maggie, I realize I've never been here with him. I've come to the parking lot to swap one truck for the other, but I don't have any idea which apartment is his.

When my call is pushed straight to voice mail again, I hesitate for only a heartbeat and call Erin.

"Hey, you," she trills, drawing each word out like she's expecting some juicy news.

I hope she's got some news instead. "Erin, have you seen Miles today? He messaged me yesterday that he'd be home last night, and I can't seem to get ahold of him." I chew on my thumbnail while watching the open stairwell closest to where his trucks are parked. Inwardly, I shudder, knowing I sound like a clingy, insecure girlfriend. *Is that what I am?* My stomach rolls at the thought that I've misread what we have. I don't *think* I have.

"He called before his flight left yesterday and debriefed me.

But I don't expect to see him in the office until next week. He told me he had something to take care of. I kind of assumed..." Her sentence trails off, but I think I know where she was headed because I'm pretty sure I assumed the same thing. "Don't worry, Chloe. He probably crashed hard from the adrenaline dump. They do that," she adds.

And I do know that. It was frustrating and hard as hell to deal with it when Dallas did that. And trying to explain to a toddler, who was equal parts excited and scared about his daddy being home... I don't even want to think about it.

"Yeah, you're right," I mumble. A shift in the blinds on a second-story window draws my attention, but the movement is so quick, so slight, that I'm not convinced I actually saw it. "His phone is just going straight to voice mail, not ringing at all."

Silence can sometimes be deafening, and Erin's is screaming into the void.

I nod, though she certainly can't see me. "Okay, well, thanks. I guess... I'll talk to you later."

Erin and I have become good friends. But she's known Miles longer; she works with him every day, poring over data and statistics. Making mission plans, extraction plans. The kind of work that requires a team to be tight and trust to be absolute.

"Chloe—"

If she knows something, there's no doubt where her loyalty lies.

"Gotta run." I disconnect and send a message to Miles.

Chloe: Missed you today. I'm going to order Chinese for dinner if you want to come over.

I glance up at the window where I thought I saw movement, but there's nothing. Not even the hint of a shadow.

ROCK, Paper, Scissors for the extra egg roll was probably a huge mistake last night. Or maybe the General Tso's chicken was a bad idea. Either way, dinner didn't sit well with me, and I feel icky. Because it certainly can't be nerves over going to the last rugby game of the season.

From the back of the car, my parents pull a tailgating tent, a table, camp chairs, a cooler, and several boxes of snacks. It's officially an end-of-season party in the Franks' tent.

"I think you might have gone a little overboard," I say as I help arrange bowls and platters on the table.

My dad huffs through his nose, and Mom laughs.

"It's a special day, Chloe. Look at how much our boy has changed since coming to the South." She stands at the edge of the rugby pitch, hands on her hips. Her cropped gingham pants, peasant blouse, and neat silver bob are such a contrast to the way she growls, "Wrap him up and take him down, Jacob." With three short claps, she turns and wanders back under the shade and fusses, "It's hotter than Hades out here. We should've brought the fan and mister. Chloe, baby, put more of those drinks on ice, would you?"

She is in her element, making a party out of my kid's rugby game. No doubt she's got enough to feed both teams and their families.

"Who's that talking to the boys?" Dad asks. "Thought you said Miles was going to be back in time for the game. Where'd he go again?"

"California." I look down the sideline and see Tyler Amarre running the team along with another boy's dad. Miles is nowhere to be seen. "He was supposed to be back, but he must've gotten caught up."

There's no doubt something is up, but I hate that I have no idea what it is. Since we've started seeing each other, not a day has gone by when we don't speak, let alone shoot a million and one messages back and forth.

Talking to Erin didn't help matters, and no matter how bad it makes me feel, as soon as the game is done, I'm going to corner Tyler and grill him for information.

ALMOST THREE DAYS.

Just shy of seventy-two hours actually.

I've officially been ghosted.

"Mom, what do we have for dessert? I'm starving."

Of course he's starving. Not even an official teenager yet, and Jake is eating me out of house and home.

"I think there are some cookies left from Nonna's rugby party yesterday," I say absently. My phone has remained disappointingly silent, though that doesn't stop me from checking it several times an hour.

Tyler had nothing to tell me after the game yesterday. Just that Miles had emailed Erin and asked if Tyler was able to fill in as coach. Erin had nothing further than that. No explanation. No information. No message.

Jake walks through the living room, one hand filled with what's likely the last of the cookies, and gives me a flyby hug. "Night, Mom."

"You're going to bed already?" I glance at my phone again and check the time. No new notifications.

"Mmhmm. Shower after I finish these and then..." The rest of his sentence is lost in a mumble around a mouthful of chocolate chip cookie.

"Don't forget to brush your teeth," I call after him.

Bronson lifts his head, ears perked forward and stubby tail twitching against my foot. I follow his gaze out the front window, hoping the headlights coming down the street pull into my driveway but they don't. Bronson puts his head down on my knee and sighs.

"I hear you, buddy." I flip his ears back, so he looks like he's got them slicked back.

My phone buzzes, and I scramble to swipe the screen and accept the call before I even check to see who it is.

Kate's nasally voice greets me, and as hard as I try to hide it, my disappointment bleeds through.

"Still MIA?" she asks.

"Yep. God, Kate, I'm sick to my stomach over this. What happened? Where is he?" I right Bronson's ears and stroke his sweet face. "What did I do?"

"Don't you dare assume you did something wrong. Men are weird creatures." She sniffs against her stuffy nose. "You didn't do anything to push him away, did you?" Only Katlyn Hays Jackson can shame me for thinking I did something wrong and then, in the next breath, ask me if I did.

"No. I mean, I don't think so," I answer, groaning as the sour feeling I've been fighting all weekend returns.

"Give me his number. I'll call him."

"What good is that going to do? Who answers calls from unknown numbers?" I whine.

Kate sneezes five times in quick succession, followed by a muttered, "Well, shit."

I can't help but laugh at my sweet, pregnant friend. Poor thing just wet her pants. "Go take care of that. I'm going to go to bed and hope I feel better in the morning."

TWENTY-FOUR

Miles

I'm too fucking old for this shit.

Never in my life would I have imagined that, at thirty-two, I'd be too old to put in a solid weekend of hard drinking and still be able to function at work on Monday morning. Or Wednesday afternoon. I honestly don't even know what day it is anymore.

"Your new phone?" Erin asks stalely.

A FedEx box lands on my desk in front of me. The thud and slide of the small box echoes through my head, a dull ache settling behind my left eye.

"Thanks," I mumble.

Any hope that Erin might take pity on me and walk on by goes to shit when she leans her hip against my desk and folds her arms over her chest. She waits patiently—or maybe not so patiently—staring me down.

"Enough of this, Clark." She nudges the box toward me.

Clearly, I'm supposed to open the thing and get it up and

functional. I palm the small rectangle of cardboard and turn it, finding a taped end. My thumbnail rhythmically scrapes across it, and I pick until a sliver of tape curls up. I pinch the free end and pull, the odd line of tape doing nothing to free the flaps of the box.

With a huff from Erin, the box flies out of my hands and reappears seconds later, empty with the contents set before me. Powered on, and the activation process started. "Are you going to finish setting this thing up, or do I need to have Chance hack your password and do it for you?"

The answer is no. I don't even want to think about the shit that would end up on my phone if those two did the setup. Porn and God knows what else from Chance, and I'm sure a tracking app from Erin.

I don't say a word. I just pull the phone toward me and tap in my email and password at each prompt. Sadly, my diligent focus on the task doesn't discourage Erin from getting comfortable. Instead, I'm treated to twenty minutes of getting my ass handed to me by my boss. And more importantly, by my friend.

"I can't keep lying for you," Erin says.

"Can't or won't?" I ask. The look on Erin's face leaves no doubt that there's little difference. With my elbows propped on my desk, splayed wide, I scrub at my face. I'm sure my overgrown beard is wild. "I never asked you to. You want to talk about me? Go right ahead. I don't give a shit, Erin. I don't fucking care."

"That's the thing." Her voice softens with concern. Concern I don't want. Concern I don't deserve. "I don't want to talk about you. I want to talk to you. With you. I want you to trust in the people around you, who care about you."

I glance up to see Jason give me a tight nod as he slips into his office. Even Chance tosses a look my way.

"Erin," I sigh heavily and throw my hands in the air, exasperated.

"You've become an important part of the team here. Fire Born Security... It's more than a job, and you know it. We're a family."

I hit her with an exaggerated slow blink and raise my brow.

"Fine. It's a fucked-up family, and we're ridiculous, embarrassing and completely inappropriate most of the time. But when things are tough or shit goes south, we're here. We've got your back, and we want to help. We just need you to be present. To talk to us." Her body is tense, eyes sternly serious, but she's leaning forward, eager, wanting me to buy in and embrace what she's saying.

"I get that, but—"

"Sometimes, superheroes need saving, too. Three days in your fortress of solitude is enough. A chapter of your life is over. It's done. That doesn't mean the whole story is. You have an amazing opportunity here, not just your job—your job is fine —but you have kids you've coached, a damsel you've saved." She pauses to let her meaning sink in. As if I could have possibly missed it. "And you have Chance."

"Chance?"

"Yep. We took a vote and decided he's your responsibility. No one else wants to hold his hair back when he pukes. You're stuck with him." She glances over her shoulder and then pins me in place again as she stands. "And I'm not your secretary. I was fine telling Tyler you needed him to coach on Saturday, but from here on out, you need to take care of your own communication. Maybe leave a little early today to weed through all your messages." With that, Erin walks away, leaving me to a killer headache and a phone bouncing across my desk with incoming notifications.

"WHAT WAS Erin all up your ass about?" Chance asks, twisting around to keep a set of perky tits in his line of sight for as long as possible.

I drag the last of my fries through a smear of ketchup and toss them in my mouth. I wash them down with the rest of my pint. "Love, support, and a little bit of *get your shit together.*"

"Just a little?" He lifts his empty glass and points to mine, wordlessly ordering us another round.

"And I guess I officially have custody of you, so you need to get your shit together, too," I say, pushing my empty plate away.

"Yeah? So, you're saying I need to find myself a nice little mommy like you did? How's that going anyway? She's sick of your sorry ass, right? That's why you're hanging out with me again." There's no subtlety in the way Chance rakes his eyes up and down our waitress when she delivers our beers. "Thanks, doll. You're free later, yeah?"

"You're a fucking pig," I say on a laugh.

"Whatever. Seriously though, you done with the single mom?"

I shrug in answer.

"So, you don't care if I step in? Take a turn and tap that?"

Fucker is making plans for tonight with the barely legal waitress and disrespecting Chloe in the same breath.

"Off-limits," I growl.

Chance flexes, rubbing a freshly inked hand over his chest,

and winks as another server passes by. "You don't want her, but no one else can have her. That's some shit right there, son. Bad fucking form." He just laughs at the scowl I throw him and continues, "I told you not to mess with the single mom, told you that was a bad idea. You went and caught feelings, both of you, and now, you're ghosting. That's fucking low class. She deserves better than that."

"Yeah, she does."

"Then, give it to her. Commit or don't, but don't fuck with her head. Or her kid's. Man up, Clark."

The time I've spent with Chance this week, the more I've realized, I hardly know him. Since when is Chance Robinson the voice of reason?

THE SCENT of fresh cut grass fills the air, and I wonder how the hell I ended up sitting in my truck, checking to see if Jake has mowed the lawn. He leans into the slight incline and stops to wipe the sweat from his face when he hits the crest.

The fact that I'm awake and out in the world this early is strictly attributable to Chance being in full mission mode last night. Not wanting anything to do with him getting his dick wet, I actually went home at a reasonable hour and got some sleep.

"Miles," Jake yells, letting the mower engine die. He bounds across the street and bounces on his toes a handful of times before catching himself and crossing his arms low over his chest. "You're finally back. Are you coming to hang out today? Mom's inside. You want me to tell her you're here, or do you wanna surprise her?" He takes a step back, his huge grin stabbing me in the heart.

"Watch it." I dash my arm out, pulling him back to the side of the truck and out of the street. "I'm not staying, just wanted to see if you were keeping up with your end of our deal."

The kid looks over his shoulder at the yard, only a few rows left to be mowed. "Uh-huh. I even trimmed the edges last week. Wanna see?"

I can see it from here, the jagged lines along the curb. "Can't. I've got to..." There is nothing I need to do today. Shifting in my seat, I pull my wallet from my back pocket and rifle through it. I pull a wad of cash out, a couple hundred bucks, and hand it to him.

Jake's brows pinch together, and his chin juts forward.

"That should cover the summer," I say, glancing at the side-view mirror of my truck.

I want to jet before Chloe wanders out. I'm managing, but if faced with seeing her, I'm pretty sure I'll crumble and beg for forgiveness. She definitely deserves better.

"So, you're done with us? What about the rules?" Disappointment winds itself around Jake as he turns away from me. His shoulders slump, making him look small and vulnerable.

I want to tell him to stand up straight, make eye contact, but any reference to the rules of being a gentleman would be hollow now. "Take good care of your mom," I say, willing him to look at me.

He doesn't. Instead, Jake takes a bracing breath, squares his shoulders, and stands tall, offering, "I will, sir. Thank you for the time you were able to give us." He thrusts his hand out, and when it's firmly grasped within my larger palm, he shakes strong and with purposeful confidence.

Watching him turn and walk away makes my chest swell with pride. He's so different from the attitude-filled, snot-nosed kid I first met months ago in the convenience store. Much as I don't want to risk seeing Chloe, I stay where I am and watch as Jake starts the mower and finishes the last strips of longer grass. He doesn't acknowledge that I'm still here as he wheels the mower to the side of the house, thoroughly cleaning it off. Not even a glance as he pushes it past me and stows it in the garage.

But when Chloe steps out onto the patio to admire his work, my heart stutters to a stop.

She looks exhausted, her skin pale, her eyes swollen and red. She hugs Jake to her, holding him tight. When she pulls back and cups his face between her hands, concern pinches her eyes. A small smile. A single nod and a kiss to his forehead, and then she turns and ushers him into the house.

The last thing I see in my rearview mirror as I drive away is Chloe leaning against the sliding glass door, a hand pressed against her stomach and the other pressed to her lips.

TWENTY-FIVE

Chloe

Tonight's dinner was way too much work for just the two of us, but my baby was sad. It was no big thing, figuring out what had taken the bounce out of Jake's step. There are only so many curvy, fully restored green '52 Chevy pickup trucks around. The muscle-clad arm, dark and messy hair and beard left no doubt about who was behind the wheel.

I held in my tears as I watched Jake's excitement at seeing Miles morph and change, settling into complete letdown. So, I did what any mama would do and scraped my sorry self up off the couch and made a roast with mashed potatoes and gravy. Fresh hot rolls and, of course, a chocolate cake.

My boy ate with gusto.

And helped clear the dishes.

And helped put away leftovers.

And then he asked if he could go up and shower before we had dessert.

He's so grown up, and yet, when I went out to tell him

what a great job he did on the lawn, he wrapped his arms around me, squeezed me tight, and was my sweet baby all over again.

While Jake's showering, I switch his mowing clothes from the washer to the dryer. The soggy wad of cash that's now spread out on the dryer is a mystery though. Twenties, tens, a handful of ones. Two hundred forty-eight dollars that I know for a fact Jake didn't have in his pocket when he went outside this morning.

"Can we have dessert in the living room, Mom?" Jake's newly acquired man smell hits my nose seconds after his feet hit the wood floor.

"We can. How big of a piece do you want?" I ask, pulling plates from the cabinet.

Jake puts his pointer fingers together, showing me how big of a wedge he wants. It's not nearly as much as I thought he'd ask for.

I cut us each a slice and drop a fork on each plate, and before I have a chance, Jake picks up both plates and carries them to the living room.

"Jake," I start but pause. I don't want to screw this up.

"Mom," he says, shoving way too much cake into his mouth at one time.

"I washed your mowing clothes."

"Mmhmm," he mumbles, a crumb clinging to his bottom lip. He loads his fork with another oversized bite.

"I found some money in the washer. Kind of a lot of money, Jake."

The cake forgotten, Jake's shoulders slump forward.

"I'm not going to be mad, I promise. But I need to know where you got that kind of money, babe." I rub my hand up the middle of his back and then hook a finger around his chin, urging him to look at me.

He sighs big and mutters, "From Miles. He promised to pay me for mowing. I thought it meant every week, like we'd keep seeing him. But..." His shoulders lift in a shrug.

"Wow. Um... Huh."

Jake flops back into the cushion. "I don't want it."

"Why? How much did he say he was going to pay you to mow the lawn?"

"Ten bucks a week." He twists his hands in the hem of his t-shirt, uncomfortable. Nervous. Full of anxiety. "It wasn't about the money, Mom. I... If I could trade it..."

It tears me apart, listening to the grown-up words spoken in his little-boy voice.

"What would you trade it for, Jake?" I run my fingers through the damp curls at the back of his head.

Sounding small, Jake whispers, "A dad."

"Oh, Jake." I pull him into my arms as his tears start to fall.

"What happened, Mom? Why did Miles go away?" He sniffs, trying so hard to be so, so big. "It's my fault, isn't it? I was... I didn't know all the rules before him. Like, the first time we met him and you fainted, I didn't know about the rules. I was rude and snotty and kind of crappy to him."

I bite back a smile at the way Jake hesitates and then emphasizes the word *crappy*. I can't imagine it's the only cuss word he uses, but the fact that he's testing it out with me makes my heart melt a little. And it's just another sign of him growing up. But the heart of what he's saying concerns me.

"And now, he's gone away and left me, too."

"What do you mean, *too*?"

"Everybody leaves me, Mom. Everybody. Daddy went

away all the time, and then he died. Uncle Jack got married to Aunt Kate, and then they had babies and moved far away. All of them left. And then Miles... I thought he liked us. I thought he was different. He..." Jake dashes a hand under his nose, sniffing hard. "He made me feel good, important. Like he cared. I thought maybe this time would be different. Like, maybe he would stay. Like, maybe we could be... like, I finally was good enough."

I shift Jake, so I can hold his face in my hands. "Good enough? For what, baby? What do you think you're not good enough for?"

His big brown eyes, which look so much like his daddy's, are glassy with tears. His bottom lip quivers as he tries so hard to hold in his emotions. His voice is so small, so vulnerable, when he says, "A dad. One who doesn't want to go away. I just want to be a family."

And with that admission, the floodgates open.

I pull Jake into my lap. He's too big, almost as tall as me, but that doesn't matter, not now, not when he's so heartbroken. Not when his world is tumbling down around him yet again.

"Oh, Jacob. None of that is your fault. Daddy died because it was his time. God had a purpose for him, and whether we understand it or not doesn't matter. He was a hero. He saved people's lives."

"I miss him, Mom. I wish he didn't have to die, but..." Jake rubs his face in my shoulder, using my t-shirt to wipe his nose.

"But what?"

"But I think he would've liked Miles. Like, I think they could've been friends, and if Dad got to pick someone to take his place and make us a family, he'd've picked Miles. Even Uncle Jack likes him. And Grandpa, too. I was trying so hard."

"Yeah." I run my fingers through his sandy curls, pushing them off his forehead. "I don't know what to say about Miles. I miss him, too. But I know for a fact that Miles didn't leave because of anything you did or didn't do. He obviously cares about you, Jake." I bury my nose in his hair and press my lips to the top of his head, breathing in the scent of body wash Miles helped Jake pick out.

Jake burrows his head into my neck, his elbow pressing into my stomach. "How do you know?" he asks softly.

"Because he came by here to check on you, baby. To make sure you were doing okay and to keep his promise to you. Maybe he's got something going on, something that he's having a hard time dealing with, but he for sure didn't want you to think he'd forgotten about your deal." They're only words. I have no idea if there's any truth to them, but with each assurance I mumble into Jake's hair, tension drains from his body. "Why don't we call it a night, babe? I'll cover our slices of cake, and we can have them for breakfast."

"Really?" With a pat to his hip and a shift of my shoulder, Jake gets the hint and sits up, staring at me.

"Really. Go on and brush your teeth."

"Love you, Mom." He squeezes me tight and lumbers up the stairs.

I wrap his cake and tuck it into the fridge, but mine, I scrape into the trash. I have no appetite. My stomach churns as I think about how much life has thrown at Jake. How much he's dealt with and just how hurt he is.

Calling Miles or even texting him is getting me nowhere. And while, initially, I was doing that for me, this is different now. When it hurts my kid, the stakes change. So, I call the only person who has been there with me through everything.

The person who caught me when the news about Dallas brought me to my knees.

"Jack, it's Chloe," I say. "Do you have a minute?"

"Hey, yeah. Just let me get Hays settled in bed." He grunts and mumbles under his breath some nonsense about his daughter being too big to be carried up the stairs.

I smile, picturing her clinging to her daddy like a baby koala. "Don't you say such things to her. Precious Hays is a princess," I coo as if I were talking directly to her instead of Jack.

"And I'm her man servant. Thank God she and her mama are going to be the only girls in this clubhouse. Hang on, Chloe."

A thud sounds from Jack putting the phone down, and then he whispers a sweet good night to one of my favorite little girls. A door creaks softly, and then Jack is back.

"So, you're excited about another boy?" I ask.

Kate had her sonogram a while ago but has been oddly tight-lipped anytime I ask her about it.

"Two boys. Twins again." He almost sounds like he feels bad about it.

"Jesus, Jack. Is Kate okay, or does she need—"

"She could probably use a shoulder to cry on and a good bottle of tequila, but she'll be fine. Deep down, I'm sure she's excited." Jack chuckles. "But I'm guessing you didn't call *me* to talk babies, so what's up?"

The sound of dishes clinking together and running water filters through the background. "God, you're such a good guy. You're doing the dishes, aren't you? And you put Hays to bed. I bet you even drew a bath for Kate, so she could relax and cry in peace over being even more overrun by testosterone in the house."

"Correct on all counts. What's going on, Chloe? Do I need to come kick Jake's ass? Get him squared away?"

"Not Jake's," I tell him.

The dishwasher door creaks, and the water tap silences. "Go on." And with those two words, Jack is in full work mode.

"Miles seems to have flaked on us, which is fine really. But Jake is feeling a little brokenhearted—more than a little—and I can't stand for that."

"Give me the rundown. Details." Ice rattles in a glass, followed by the glug and splash of what's most likely some of the high-end tequila he and Kate adore.

With a deep, bracing breath, I tell Jack what's up, focusing on the events of the past week. That everything seemed to be going fine, that Miles and I made plans for when he returned from California. How he ghosted. And then—because, really, it's the most important part—how he broke my kid. When I hear myself relay the events aloud, it doesn't seem all that bad. That is, until I think of Jake crying in my arms and trying his hardest not to.

"I know I'm being a girl about this, but—"

"Not at all. Individually, yeah, it's shit. But considering what he's been working on and then the final kick in the junk, it kind of makes sense."

My head is spinning. Jack doesn't cut anyone slack. Ever. But this goes beyond just giving Miles a pass. "What do you know, Jack? Did you... Did you look into him? Jesus, really?"

He scoffs like that's a ridiculous question. "Of course I did. Don't act like that surprises you. You know I would never sit back and watch you give your heart to anyone without knowing what kind of person they were. What kinds of skeletons were in their closets. And I'm not saying Miles is handling things all that great on his end, but maybe give him a pass this time. A week isn't all that long for him to make peace with his shit."

"What is Miles handling? What's he been working toward? What does he need to make peace with?" My heart is racing, and my stomach rolls over on itself, making me wonder yet again if I'm going to need to run for the bathroom and bow before the porcelain throne.

"His trip to California. He didn't mention what he was going for?"

"I mean, I knew he was going. I knew it was weighing heavy on him, but this is what you guys do. You go into shitty situations and save the world. You don't talk about it outside of the circle of trust. Then, you come home to your families, and we get to try to make things better—normal—again. But he didn't come home to me, Jack. I'm not comparing this to how Dallas left us, to how we lost him, but Miles didn't come home to me. And now, there's no finality. He's here, in town. He stopped by but didn't see me, didn't talk to me, just got Jake all kinds of upset. And, God, he sobbed, soaked my shirt with snot and tears, just like... like when..." My heart twists painfully as I think back to the morning I told my little boy his daddy was never coming home to us.

"Chloe, you need to flip this one around. Go to Miles. Talk to him."

"Tell me what's going on. I can't walk into this blind. You guys are the heroes, not me."

"I'll call your parents, have them come get Jake for the day, maybe a couple days—"

"We still have school, Jack. We can't just blow that off," I say, but I'm already doing a quick rundown of my lesson plans for the first half of the week. I can make it work and take some time.

"Is Miles important to you? Do you..."

"Love him?" I ask and then sigh. "I do. Yeah, I do." I hate that I don't say the words to Miles first.

"Then, go to him. Make him talk to you. Make him understand that you're there for him. That you're not going anywhere," Jack says.

Whatever is going on, it's serious. Gravely serious by the tone of Jack's voice.

"He's a good guy, Chloe. And he needs you. He's going to push you away—hard—but you gotta stick with him."

"Jack, you're freaking me out."

"Don't. Just... I think he needs you to put him back together."

TWENTY-SIX

Miles

I don't know how many days have slipped past. How many hours I've spent numb. How many bottles of whiskey are lying empty in the trash. If someone hadn't loaded them all into a bag and thrown them away, I'd at least be able to count them up. Or try to.

As it is, I'm exhausted.

How long can I do this?

How many days can I drink away before I officially have a problem?

An annoying voice in the back of my head whispers that I'm probably already there.

It's been like a goddamn parade through here for the last... I don't even know. Calvin called to check in on me. Jason tried, too, but when he didn't get anywhere, Erin showed up at my door. She talked. Said all the things she was supposed to. That it wasn't my fault. I did everything I could. I went above and beyond what anyone could have expected of me. I gave my all.

That's where shit went sideways. I fought her on everything she said. And with nothing left to say, every heartfelt statement twisted into a meaningless platitude for me to cast off, she conceded. Erin, one of my best friends, walked out the door.

Was that yesterday? The day before?

I peel myself off the cheap leather couch, leaving a layer of skin behind. I stink. I need a shower and food and a run.

An impatient fist pounds on the door, no pause between each series of head-splitting raps.

I stumble across the apartment and pull open the door, a simple, "Fuck," falling from my lips.

"What do you want?" I grumble at Chance. "You here to blow sunshine up my ass, too? Don't waste your time."

I swing the door shut and turn away, wondering if I have anything to eat. Tacos and homemade guac would be fucking stellar right now.

"Fuck that. I have no interest in your ass or blowing anything." Chance saunters through the door, letting it close with a bang.

"Then, why are you here? I'm on leave—vacation." I snort a laugh at the thought. This is no fucking vacation. It's a goddamn nightmare. "Anything you need for my project, Erin knows where to access it."

"Nope. Couldn't give a shit about work right now either." He flops down on the couch I just vacated and wrinkles his nose as he looks around at my mess.

I rifle through the fridge and come out with a couple of beers. There's not much else in there, so I'm going to have to sweet-talk him into driving my sorry ass to the liquor store. If that's not a sign that I've fallen pretty far down the hole, I don't know what is.

"This is all I've got." I toss a can to him, but Chance looks at the label and sets it down on top of a pile of unopened mail on the table.

"No, thanks. So, uh, where you at with the chick?" He leans back and runs his hand over his stubble, the rasp echoing in the silence.

I slam my can of beer on the counter, foam bubbling out and running down my clenched hand. "The fuck, man? She's dead. Where do you think I'm at?" I want to punch the stupid look off his face.

"The single mom? So, does that make you... like, the kid's not your responsibility or anything, right?" He looks almost as confused as I feel.

"What? No, not Chloe. She's... I'm sure she's fine." She has to be. I need her to be okay.

Chance waves a hand, brushing me off. "So, the mommy, she's fair game? You done with her?"

"Yeah, we're done."

"Sweet. I'mma tap that ass, then. Figure if you're this broken up, she's got to be worth a little effort," he says, neck cracking loudly as he twists his head.

Chance stands, and before he can take a step for the door, before he can even think of doing it, I am in his face. Shoulders back, chest puffed out, jaw tight as shit.

"The fuck you will, motherfucker. The. Fuck. You. Will." Voice low, threat apparent, I clench my free hand into a tight fist, ready to lay him out. "Chloe is off-limits, you hear me? Not just no, but hell no. Fuck no. No." I step in closer, ready to tear him limb from limb for talking about Chloe that way. Ready to murder the heartless bastard for daring to even think about touching her. "Do you fucking hear me?" I demand, glowering.

And Chance smiles. He takes a step back, putting some separation between us, and nods. His slicked-back hair doesn't move from the motion. "Loud and clear, my friend. Loud and fucking clear." He slaps the front of my shoulder as he passes, hard enough to push me out of his way. "Get your shit sorted and get back to work, man. I'm tired of covering for your ass."

Chance walks out the door, and I'm left rooted to my spot, beer in hand, wondering when the fuck he became the responsible one.

No sooner has the door slammed shut behind him than a quick, loud rap sounds against it. At least it feels like it happens in quick succession. I seriously have no sense of time right now. I could have been standing here for a minute or twenty, but by the chill on the beer can still clasped in my hand, it couldn't have been all that long. Fucker probably decided to come back for a drink after all.

I swing the door open without even looking and turn to stumble back to the couch. My moment of sobriety fueled by anger has passed. I just want to sink into my shitty couch and drink myself to sleep.

"Forget something, asshat?" I say, my eyes already closing.

I should put my half-empty beer down before it falls out of my hand, but I don't. I'll just clean up the mess in the morning. Or not. Who gives a shit?

The can slips a little, my grip going lax as my body gets heavy with sleep.

"The fuck you want, Tin Man?" I mumble, not even sure Chance is still here.

The door softly clicks shut.

"Miles?"

I peel my eyes open because either Chance's balls are in a vise or it's not him in my apartment. That voice is too high. Too sweet. Too... too *Chloe.*

"What're you doing here?" I try to push myself up to sitting, but it takes some serious concentration before I can make it happen. "How'd you... You've never..." I rub a hand down my face, trying to clear my head and figure out how she knew which apartment was mine. We spent all our time at her house, the beach, but not here.

"Erin. I had an idea of where it was, but I begged her for the number, so I wouldn't knock on the wrong door." She takes a tentative step in and looks around at my sparse furnishings. Her gaze bounces around, taking in the nothingness of my apartment. Couch. TV. Coffee table. It looks more like a long-term efficiency rental than the place someone's lived in for almost a year.

I let her look though. Because while she's focused elsewhere, I get to focus on her. The black hair tumbling down her back, free from its binds for a rare moment. Her sparking blue eyes, clear, concerned. The pout of her pink lips pulled down at the corners. She's fresh-faced and beautiful. I stare at her for as long as possible, memorizing all the tiny details that I've missed.

Her gaze swings back to meet mine, and after a beat, I look away.

"We had an agreement," Chloe says, taking the few steps to the end of the couch. She lowers herself to perch on the edge of the cushion by my feet, the shitty excuse for leather squeaking as she sits. "You broke it."

Jesus, fuck, going right for the kill, isn't she?

"I guess I did." I let my head sink into the cushion behind me and close my eyes. It's easier to let her go, to push her away, if I don't have to see her.

"It goes against the rules."

My mouth twists. "What?"

"You take the time to coach a bunch of boys in a stupidly violent-looking game. You hold them to a standard and teach them what it means to be a gentleman. To keep their word, be respectful, make eye contact." She pauses, waiting for me to do just that but I don't. I can't. "And then you ignore it all yourself."

There's nothing I can say. I can't dispute any of what she said.

"Will you talk to me, please? Look at me, Miles. Just look at me and tell me what happened. What changed so drastically with us?"

How can I explain it to her? How do I tell her that I thought I had everything and lost it? Only to find it again in her and Jake—a family. One I almost lost and then begged, pleaded for, so I could have the honor of keeping them, all based on the promise that there would be no secrets. And I've been keeping a big fucking secret I can't even deal with.

Her head dips forward, and she gathers her hair, twisting it into a braid over one shoulder, like she did so many months ago on Erin and Blake's deck. Silence stretches between us, layering itself on top of tension and secrets and lies of omission. I'm stubborn. Angry. Barely functioning. But for the life of me, I know I can't look her in the eye, see the sadness there.

"I know it's big, whatever happened. I know it's bad. But more than anything I know that I want to help you. That I don't want to lose you.

"Erin only gave me your apartment number. Jack—Dallas's best friend—he knows but isn't sharing. God, you have so many people who love you, who want to help, who want to support you and heal you and help you find a way to put yourself back together. I love you, Miles. I never thought I'd feel that again after losing Dallas. Never for a minute thought I'd find someone who could fill the hole he left in my life."

She reaches out, placing her delicate hand on mine, and I flinch. I fucking flinch, and she pulls away, which is stupid because every cell in my body is reaching for her, yearning for her. I want to wrap myself up in her. Let her be the binds that hold me together.

I dare to take a glance at her. A shaky sigh deflates her shoulders, curling them inward. With a nod, Chloe reaches into her bra and pulls out a folded stack of bills. Clasped in her lap, she briefly fiddles with them and then places them on the coffee table. Then, Chloe stands and walks to the door.

"What is that for? Is that the money I gave Jake?" I can't stop myself from looking at her now. It happens without any thought, any control.

With her back to me, Chloe pauses. "It is."

"Take it back. It's his for—"

"He doesn't want it, Miles. Money isn't what he was looking for."

I lean forward, elbows on my knees, head in my hands. "He can buy whatever he wants." I pick up the cash and hold it out. When she doesn't take it, barely even glances back at it, I toss it to the other end of the table, bills fanning out. "Just take it."

Chloe turns to face me, moving so fast that it almost makes me seasick—and I don't fucking get seasick. Her face is angry, all kinds of red. "Don't you get it? He doesn't want your fucking money. He can't buy what he wants."

The fact that she dropped the fuck-word surprises me, but I snag my wallet off the coffee table and rifle through. There's no cash. I gave it all to Jake earlier, and it's sitting right there. I pull out a credit card. "Here. Take this. I don't care how much he spends, max it out. Get him whatever he wants." I stand and take a step toward her, my arm extended.

"I can't. That's not how it works."

"Then, what does he want?"

"A family. And foolish or naive or whatever, over the past couple of months, it wasn't just me who fell in love with you, but my kid did, too. He thought you genuinely cared about him." She bats at the tears that have spilled over, trailing down her cheeks. "I'm hurt, devastated, but I've gotten over heartbreak once before, and I can do it again. My kid though? He lost the man who taught him how to *be* a man. And he's pretty sure it's all his fault."

Chloe opens the door and walks through it, letting it slam behind her, the sound punctuating exactly how alone I am.

Jesus Christ, what have I done?

TWENTY-SEVEN

Chloe

I stumble down the stairs, tears burning my eyes. I know Jack said to fight for Miles, to make him talk to me and tell me what he's battling against, but I won't force him to let me in. He has to want it. Want us.

It takes all of two minutes to drive the four blocks home, and when I get there, I almost wish that Jake were here instead of with my parents. With the house empty, my heart bruised and battered, I feel more exposed inside than I do blanketed by the warm night air.

I pad through the kitchen and push out the back door, Bronson trailing after me. The soft glow of little landscape lights acts as a beacon, drawing me to the garden. I settle on the bench that a husband made by hand for his wife. The one that Miles took my child to get for me for Mother's Day.

Bronson checks the yard and then comes back and curls up at my feet, and my toes automatically rub against his belly. As soothing as it is for him, it's just as much of a balm to me.

We'll be okay.

As the wind picks up, promising a coming storm, I allow myself to cry, cycling through the stages of grief. I don't really even know if those apply to this mess. I'm sure, if I felt like digging in and doing the work that my therapist encouraged years ago as I processed the loss of Dallas, I'd find that they do, that I can make my feelings fit into a box and file them away. But I don't want to.

Instead, I let the tears flow, unchecked, down my face.

And tomorrow, I'll figure out if I want to wallow in this messy place or pick myself up and get shit done.

Bronson lifts his head, staring into the silence. He doesn't growl, just focuses squarely on the side of the house, where the gate is.

Miles emerges from the darkness and soundlessly makes his way across the yard. Hands shoved deep in the pockets of his shorts, his head hanging, chin practically resting on his chest.

He clears his throat and blows out a deep breath. I can almost hear him counting the hold before he inhales slowly.

"My daughter was barely a month old when my wife killed her."

Air rushes from my lungs in a searing whoosh.

"I found them. Walked in the door and found Aly clutching a knife by the blade, blood running down her hand and dripping from the bottom of the bassinet. She'd be two now. Walking, talking, all of that, but she's gone, never got the chance."

He shifts his weight and continues, "Aly didn't do well with the pregnancy. She, uh... she suffered with depression. A lot. But the doctors were there. They were on top of things, checking in, monitoring her. No one saw her break coming.

They had no idea that she was hiding not just postpartum depression, but also a full PPD psychosis."

My hands fly to my cheeks, finally pushing away the tears I shed for my broken heart, only to make room for fresh ones for Miles's loss.

"My team was gearing up, doing mission prep, and I... I was gone a lot. Working long hours, focused on the upcoming mission." His shrug is a barely there movement, more of a shift than an actual lift of his shoulder. "I got scrubbed from the mission and placed on watch. Buried my daughter. Saw a therapist and tried to figure out how to live. It was a lot—honestly too much. I fought myself with feelings of failure. In my job, as a father, a husband. I was a mess for a while.

"I finally figured out that I had to do something, so I took as much leave as I could and decided to separate from the navy. Thank God, Calvin—the guy who started Fire Born Security—hired me. I don't know if it was pity or what, but as much as I'd like to think I was getting my shit together at that point..." The grimace that twists his face finishes the thought better than words.

Miles sucks in a lungful of air and then blows it out his nose, preparing for whatever he has to say next. "I'm not proud of it because I knew she was sick, but the first thing I did was divorce my wife. The DA took that, ran with it at trial, and pushed for the harshest penalty for Aly. There was a lot of guilt with that." He shifts his weight, maybe swaying a little, his head hanging low. Shame and guilt draped over him.

"Miles, I'm so sorry. I don't know what to say. Is... is that why you went to California? Not for work, but to see..." I don't know how to address her. Aly? His wife? The woman who took what he'd obviously held very dear?

He lifts his head and briefly meets my eyes before tilting it up to the sky, a quick flash of lightning illuminating his strong profile. "Yeah. While the DA was pushing for a sentence of life in prison, I worked closely with her doctors, family, her legal team to have her placed in a long-term facility. What she'd done was awful, beyond my worst nightmare, but she was sick. Prison wouldn't give her the kind of mental health care she needed, so I did everything in my power to help her get just that."

Thunder rumbles in the distance.

"Did it not... Your message when you were leaving Cali sounded like whatever you were there for was a success. Did I read that wrong? I mean, obviously, I thought it was work stuff, but I thought—"

"No," he says, gently cutting me off. "You're right. It was all good. When I left California, she was being transported to her new facility, but by the time I landed here, she'd taken her own life."

I can't help the gasp that shoots from my lungs, the sound of it loud in the still night.

"Yeah, I know. I did everything I could to make things right. To make sure that another life wasn't lost to Aly's illness. It baffled the prosecutors on her case. I lobbied *for* her, not against. Begged for her to get help, not just be locked away. And I failed. Again."

"Miles, you didn't fail—"

He hums in disagreement maybe. "But I did. I *feel* like I did, even more so now that she's gone. You know, I worked through all the stages of grief. I took a lot of my initial anger out on Maggie and—"

"Your truck?"

He laughs, quick and with more resignation than humor. "Yep. I poured myself into restoring her, finding and fixing every little thing, stripping her down and building her up. And at the same time, I put myself back together. I know it sounds stupid, but working on that truck saved me. And when she was done and Calvin saw me struggling again, he suggested taking a position here, starting over fresh." He gives me a tight smile.

We both came here to start over. To move on from losses so big, so life changing. Two tattered hearts seeking salvation.

"And I did. I found happiness I hadn't thought I'd find again. A job that's, God, the next best thing to what I was doing as a SEAL. Still fulfilling but without the deployments, without the part that I blamed for missing Aly's spiral. And when things felt good, really good, you fell into my arms. You and Jake"—he glances around my little yard—"all of this, gave me the pieces I had been missing. A family. It was all perfect, almost too good to be true. So, when Ryan—Aly's lawyer—called to tell me she was gone, that she'd taken her life..."

Warm drops of rain fall, landing on the top of my head like tender kisses. Wet dots bloom on the bench, raindrops getting fatter and falling harder as each second ticks by.

"Come inside," I say, rising to my feet. I grasp Miles's hand, guiding him toward the house.

"I should go." He tugs on his hand, but there's no way I'm going to let him go. Not now, not after all that he told me.

I lead him into the kitchen, and as if it were waiting for us, the sky opens up as the door shuts behind us. In the bright glow of the overhead light, Miles looks even worse than he did at his apartment. Eyes bloodshot, hair and beard wild. His clothes rumpled, splotches of rain darkening his t-shirt.

"Go sit down," I tell him, waving a hand to quiet him when he starts to protest.

I grab a glass of water and ease down on the couch, Miles parked in the center, elbows resting on his strong thighs.

"Drink this and then finish what you were going to say. The lawyer called you," I prompt, handing him the glass.

Miles quickly drains it, setting it on the table when he's done. "Yeah, all the ways I failed Aly and the baby hit me like a punch to the gut. I couldn't breathe. I couldn't think. It was like a warning to let you and Jake go before I failed you more than I already had." Exhaustion dragging him down, Miles slumps back into the downy cushions.

"How do you think you failed us, Miles?"

He tenses briefly. "The bench, the robbery. I put Jake in danger, and you could have lost him. It would've been my fault; I'd have taken him from you. I know what that feels like, Chloe. I'd rather bear the pain of losing you both, knowing you were safe without me, than to have you suffer that loss. But turns out"—he turns his head, so his hazy brown gaze is directed right at me—"I don't think I can live without you guys. I love you so goddamn much, it hurts. I'm tired of pain. So fucking tired of it."

I reach out, placing my palm on his cheek, my thumb stroking his whiskers away from his lips.

"I love you," Miles repeats, his lips moving against my thumb. "I don't want to lose you."

I press my lips to his temple and pull his body toward me, settling his torso between my thighs and his head against my stomach. Almost immediately, Miles's breathing evens out, his face going slack with sleep. I trace his dark, heavy brows before trailing my fingers across his cheekbones and down his nose.

Did his daughter look like him? Did her mouth purse in sleep with the perfect cupid-bow lips, like his? Or did he see his wife—ex-wife—every time he looked at her? How did he get up each morning and get through his day, not showing any of that pain to the world?

The press of his weight, his warmth, the soft and even puff of breath at each exhale act together, relaxing me. The drumming beat of the rain pelting against the window finally pulls me under, exhaustion consuming me.

TWENTY-EIGHT

Miles

While Chloe forgave me for being a dumbass, Jake has been a much harder sell. I don't blame him one bit for the attitude he gives me. Actions speak louder than words, and I shit all over the relationship we'd forged.

Even with strict adherence to the rules I spent months teaching him, I haven't made a ton of progress. As May starts its downward slide, I've got to do something to mend the rift I created.

"Jake, you want to come with me and grab some ice cream?"

Chloe made a big dinner but accidentally forgot to make dessert at my request.

"Mom doesn't like ice cream, or did you forget?" And there's that attitude he was full of when we met.

Chloe huffs out a laugh. "I'm stuffed, babe. You and Miles go on without me, and I'll get these dishes done." She throws me a wink and mouths a silent, *Good luck.*

"Come on." I give his shoulder a light squeeze as I grab my keys from the counter.

Jake drags his feet but follows me out to Maggie, sliding into the passenger seat as Bronson hops on the bench seat between us. "Damn it, Bronson." He doesn't bother using one of his substitute curses, but now is not the time for me to correct that.

"Jake, I need to apologize to you. What I did, the way I dropped out of your mom's life and yours, that wasn't right. I struggle with making excuses for myself, almost as much as I struggle with accepting them from others."

He peers at me from behind Bronson's back, brows lowered, his thinking face on.

"But people make mistakes. Sometimes, those mistakes are innocent, and sometimes, they're intentional but with good intent, no ill will. Does that make sense?"

He nods, so I continue, wanting to explain this as best I can, "I was married before, a couple of years ago, way before I met you guys."

"When you were a SEAL?"

I pull into a space at the ice cream shop and park. "Yep. My wife was..." I sigh, bracing myself. Weighing my words. "She did something bad, something very serious, that resulted in another person's death."

"She killed someone? She was a murderer?" There's no hiding the shock leaching into his voice or painted on his face.

"She did kill someone, but it's kind of hard to explain. She was sick."

"So, she murdered because she was sick?"

Shock turns to confusion—and isn't that the fucking thing? I don't want to give him so many details that he's scarred from it. I carry enough of that myself. But I want to do the explanation justice—at least, as much as I can.

"She suffered from a mental illness, and at the time, she didn't know what she was doing. It was wrong, very wrong.

"When I went to California, I went there to talk to the judge and the lawyers. I wanted to help her get the care that she needed. Unfortunately, the sickness was too strong, too much, and she died."

Chloe and I talked at length about how much to tell Jake, what to tell him and how to say it. I don't know whether it's right or wrong to fudge the details of exactly how Aly died, but for the sake of an eleven—almost twelve—year-old, boy, we decided to censor this particular detail.

Jake's hand goes to Bronson's back, stroking his fur as he processes what I shared. "Miles, who did she kill?" he asks softly.

Part of me hoped that he wouldn't ask, but this, I won't gloss over. That would feel too wrong. "Our daughter."

Sadness pulls at the corners of Jake's eyes, and he sniffs quietly, chewing at his lip. "I'm sorry she did that. I'm sorry you don't have a kid anymore."

"Thank you. That means a lot. I'm still her dad, even though she's not here. Just like you will always have your dad."

I pause, letting that thought sink in for both of us.

"So, that's what happened, and that's why I was really sad —pretty mad, too—and I was afraid of losing you and your mom. Afraid enough to push you guys away, thinking it would be easier for everyone, but I was really wrong. And if you'll forgive me, I'd like to be part of your lives again."

He picks at his lower lip and sniffs noisily. "I would like that. A lot."

"There's one last thing I need to clear with you before we go get dessert. And if it wasn't super important, I would never ask you to keep a secret from your mom, not for anything, but I would like to ask her to marry me. I want to make sure that it's okay with you first though." I hold my breath because, honestly, I'm going to ask her; it'll just be that much easier if Jake is on board.

A smile lights up his face, and he asks, "Really?"

I match his smile and nod.

Jake thrusts his hand toward me to shake and says, "Welcome to the family."

I shake his hand, ignoring his clamminess from wiping away snot, proud of the way he's handled something a kid should never have to hear about.

"SO, is there something special you two do for Father's Day?" I ask.

With a quick, shrill whistle, Bronson trots across the yard and into the house, splaying out on the AC vent in the corner of the kitchen.

"What do you mean?" Chloe lifts the dishwasher door with her heel and bumps it shut. "I thought you were cool with going to my parents'."

"I am. Just... Do you do something special to honor Dallas?" I've worked hard over the past couple of weeks, proving myself to Jake, building trust, and earning his respect again. "I don't want to be in the way, so I can just cut out for a bit, let you guys do your thing, and then swing back when you're ready to go."

Chloe folds the dish towel, neatly tucking it in the laundry room. She stands with a hip resting against the counter, arms folded across her chest, pushing her boobs together. "Before we moved, we'd go visit Dallas's grave, and then, we'd just hang out for the rest of the day. Nothing we can really replicate here." Sadness flashes in her eyes before she covers it with a smile. "What about you? I should have asked before now, but is there something special you do?"

We still tiptoe around discussions of Aly and my daughter —mostly Aly. Chloe is hugely supportive of me when I talk about them, but it's never an easy discussion. For any of us.

"I'll talk to my dad at some point, but I don't know. I haven't really thought about it."

She seems to think about that, her brows pulling together, but the subject dies right there for the night.

IN THE MORNING, after a quick detour for doughnuts and coffee and a chocolate milk, we make the drive out into the country. Chloe's parents live in a big house on a good-sized chunk of land.

"Uncle Brent and Uncle Drew are going to be there, right?" Jake asks from the backseat.

"Yep." Chloe smirks at me from the passenger seat.

While her parents seem to like me just fine, she's hinted at the fact that her older brothers can be kind of brutal.

"And Uncle Jack won't, right? Did we send him a card?"

"We?" Chloe glances in the backseat and laughs at Jake's shocked expression. "Yes, *we* sent Jack a card and Grandpa Triplett, too. I covered all your bases for you."

"Almost all of them," Jake mumbles under his breath,

leaning forward and most likely thinking only Chloe can hear him.

The rest of the drive is quiet, uneventful, but with aunts and uncles, cousins and grandparents, chaos fills our day.

Over grilled burgers and more salads and desserts than a group our size needs, gifts are handed out.

Chloe's big, bad brothers might think they're tough. But when Brent puts on the pink construction-paper tie with unicorn stickers decorating it, his street cred dies a painful death.

"Don't you look pretty?" Drew drawls, winking at his brother.

Brent smooths down his paper tie, nodding at the play makeup set Drew just unwrapped. "Prettier than you'll be, even after your makeover."

A tiny version of Drew's wife climbs up onto his lap, digging into the makeup crap and swiping pink and blue powder across his face. It hits me that she's about the age my daughter would be. I allow myself just a moment to imagine her playing dress-up with me, and I smile.

"Don't laugh, man. She's been eyeing your beard since you got here, and I've got some bows in my princess kit here," Drew razzes me.

"That's a hard pass," I say.

Jake leans over to Chloe and whispers, his hand cupped around his mouth. She nods, and he bounces from his seat and trots over to the tote bag she tucked under the small table by the door. He hands Chloe's dad a card and then hands me a royal-blue gift bag, bright red tissue sticking out the top.

"Happy Father's Day," he says, cheeks turning red as everyone watches.

"What's this?" I ask, looking from Jake to Chloe and back.

"It's just... Nothing. I thought..."

I pluck the tissue from the bag and pull out a blue compression shirt, a red Superman symbol on the chest. "Thanks, Jake." I unfold the shirt, and a keychain in the shape of a green '52 Chevy pickup clatters to the table. "And you got something for Maggie, too. Thank you."

I pull him in for a hug, giving him an extra squeeze and then a pat on the shoulder. Jake nods, red creeping higher on his cheeks as he shuffles off into the house.

My throat tightens with emotion, and Chloe reaches over, threading her fingers through mine.

WE GET HOME LATE ENOUGH that Jake climbs straight up the stairs and into the shower.

"Thank you for today," I say, wrapping my arms around Chloe from behind. With my nose, I push her loose strands of hair to the side and place a kiss to the nape of her neck. Goose bumps pop up, dotting the skin across her shoulders. "The shirt and keychain were perfect."

Chloe turns in my arms, twisting her fingers in the hair at the back of my head. She scrapes her nails down my neck, causing my skin to tighten, the same as hers. "That was all Jake. He thought them up and picked them out. I just played secretary and did the ordering."

"Well, shit."

"Exactly. Puts you in a pretty elite club. I think that's the only Father's Day gift he's even had any input on."

Chloe slides her hands around to my neck, scraping her

nails through my beard. I should probably make a point to trim it soon. It's getting a bit unruly.

My dick stirs as she dances her fingers across my shoulders and down my pecs, circling my nipples.

"You got a little something for me, too?" I palm her ass and press her tight into my hips, blood flooding south.

As much as I love spending time with her family, I would give my right nut to sneak Chloe out to the beach house one of the guys at work has and bury myself in her for a solid week, no interruptions.

"I do. A couple of things actually," Chloe says, pinching my left nipple.

My dick is well beyond stirring and fucking begs for her after that. She runs a hand over the front of my shorts, giving me a playful squeeze before sauntering away from me.

I follow her up the stairs, admiring the sultry sway of her hips. In the bedroom, she rummages around in the closet for a hot minute before returning to me. Her tits sway alluringly, free from the bra she obviously took a few magical seconds to shed while she was in there, a square box resting in her palms.

"What's this?" I ask, taking the footlong square box from her, though honestly, I'd rather finish unwrapping her than get to whatever's in this box.

"Remember that surprise I borrowed Maggie for on Mother's Day weekend?" She taps the top of the box a couple of times with her finger and bites her lip.

"I do. Guess with Jake spilling about our adventures that day, I forgot all about it." I resist the temptation to shred the box, instead slipping my fingers into the cardboard to pry it open.

My breath leaves in a rush.

"Sweet baby Jesus, woman, what have you done?" I lift an image of Chloe set in a simple black frame from the box. Full pinup. Glossy black waves. Ruby-red lips. Tight skirt, white blouse flashing a hint of red lace, fuck-me shoes to match, and goddamn seams up the backs of her hose.

I can barely form words.

"There's more," she says, her voice husky with desire.

I dig through the box, pulling two more frames out—same outfit, different poses. All fucking knockouts.

"The album has a few more."

I don't even look. Because I have the real thing, in the flesh, here to touch, taste, and love any damn time I want, just as long as she says yes.

I fully planned to do the whole thing—dress up, dinner, drop to my knee after a million pretty words, and ask her to be my wife. But I don't want to wait. I reach in my pocket, slip the ring from the black velvet box, and slide it onto her finger.

"As beautiful as I'm sure every one of those pictures is, I won't be able to appreciate the artistry behind them right now. I love you, Chloe. I don't want to think of what my life would be like without you. Marry me. Make me the happiest man on earth."

"Yes," just barely breaches her lips before my mouth crashes into hers.

EPILOGUE

Ensign Jacob Wyatt Triplett
Graduate, United States Naval Academy
Annapolis, Maryland

Twelve Years Later

It doesn't take long for me to find my family in the crowd. All of them and then some. Mom and Miles are the first ones I see—two of my little sisters tucked in tight between them, I'm sure. Gramps and Nonna smile and chat with Grandma and Grandpa Triplett. Well, mostly, Nonna does the smiling and chatting. Gramps is standing tall, proud as fuck after witnessing his only grandson graduate from a service academy.

That's the limit of my seating allotment for the ceremony. It's actually over, but I wouldn't put it past Miles to smuggle the littlest of my sisters in.

I owe him.

Big.

The lessons I learned from him on life, love, and what it

means to be a man are what got me here. Not just here as in my appointment to and graduation from the naval academy, but here as in who I am.

I glance toward the sky, the sun strong on my face, and say a silent thanks to my dad. He'd be proud as fuck too, though I have no doubt that since his blood ran army green, he'd give me hell for choosing the navy.

And like my dad is sitting on a cloud in heaven, dropping people where he wants them for maximum personal entertainment, Uncle Jack's gruff voice sounds behind me. "Jesus Christ, the last place I ever thought I'd piss away a perfectly good Saturday in May is surrounded by a bunch of newly minted ensigns."

I spin on my heel and nod crisply. "Sir. Aunt Kate. Thank you for being here today. It means the world to me."

"Oh my God, I can't believe you're old enough for this." Aunt Kate pulls me into an over-the-top hug, and I stiffen, trying uselessly to pull away.

"Jake's still on a short leash until he's out of uniform, Kate. Don't get him reprimanded the minute he graduates. Give him a minute." Uncle Jack looks around and nods to where my mom is struggling to make her way through the throng of people without losing everybody. "Besides, he's probably got a much younger model than you he'd rather get in trouble for."

I huff out a laugh. "No, sir, I do not."

I could have a girl. In fact, I've had several. This uniform is like catnip, and pussy tends to be ripe for the taking. But that's not a conversation I plan on having with them.

"Will you be joining us for lunch?" I ask. Anything to direct the subject away from the action I've been getting.

Uncle Jack nods and glances behind him, a huge grin

sliding across his face. "Absolutely. Now that the stragglers have decided to show up. You find what you need, sugar?"

He reaches past Aunt Kate and wraps his arm around his daughter, protectively pulling her into his side. And it's a damn good thing he does because, at seventeen, Hays Margaret Jackson is most definitely the younger, hotter—*much hotter*—version of her mother.

For the love of fucks, when did that happen?

"Hays," I say, nodding my head. "Mason. Dix," I greet her older brothers with a handshake. "Where are the littles?"

"Hotel pool with Mom's parents. Dad could only sneak so many of us in," Mason replies.

Hays smiles, her big brown eyes taking in the sea of crisp navy-and-white uniforms around her. "Hey."

My family and all the grands finally make it down onto the field and fall into easy conversation, catching up and relaying plans. And I just want to get out of my hot uniform and suck down a beer with a lunch *not* from the mess hall.

A hard slap lands on my shoulder, and Ben Levy—my first friend in Virginia and roommate for my final semester—slides into our not-so-little circle.

"Ben, congratulations, sweetie," Mom says. "Were your parents able to make it back stateside?"

For all four years we were at the academy, Ben's parents were stationed overseas. With us two being close and Mom and Miles being who they are, Ben has spent a lot amount of time with my family. Holidays, breaks. Football games. He just fits right in.

"No, ma'am. They were delayed leaving and won't be in until sometime tomorrow," he says.

"Oh, I'm sorry. Join us for lunch." She relays the plans and then turns her attention to Aunt Kate and Hays, making a big thing over how much Hays has changed since she saw her last.

She's not wrong. I think the last time I saw Hays was the Christmas before I graduated high school. She was skinny and awkward, her nose stuck in a book, her smile glinting with metal.

"Who's that?" Ben asks under his breath. "Jesus, she is fine."

I follow his line of sight and bristle when I see he's homed in on Hays. Her tits actually—and those for sure were not at all a thing the last time I saw her.

"Back off, dickless," I growl.

Ben raises his brows, his smirk firmly in place as he checks her out from head to toe.

Mason notices and squares his shoulders, unmistakable military bearing in his stance.

"You laying claim? Gonna tap that round ass to celebrate being done with this shit for a while?" Ben is not nearly as quiet or subtle as he thinks he is, and both Mason and Dixon bristle at the way he's talking about their sister. Their baby sister.

I turn Ben, guiding him far enough away for our conversation to remain private. "Seriously, lay off. She's seventeen, not even legal, and we're practically family. She's like a sister to me." The words don't feel right in my mouth.

I mean, I've known Hays her entire life. Saw her every year, at least once a year, until I started at USNA. But she has changed.

"Sister, huh?" Ben mumbles. "Stepsister maybe."

It doesn't even register that I've moved until my fist connects with his jaw.

Hays may not be mine, but I won't let anyone talk about her like that.

Thank you for choosing to spend your valuable time reading **Tattered Hearts.** I would be so honored if you'd take a moment to leave a review on your favorite retail platform.

To stay up to date on releases, sales, and happenings, please subscribe to my newsletter at www.kcenderswrites.com

RULES OF BEING A GENTLEMAN

Say Please & Thank you
Work hard
Mind your manners
Don't curse
Offer a lady your seat
Extend a firm handshake
Keep your word
Respect your elders
Always make eye contact
Be punctual
Open doors for others
Stay well groomed
Stand up straight
Shy away from gossip
Read books often

WRITING PLAYLIST

Rock Bottom - Grandson
Lie – NF
Broken – The People's Thieves
The Jester – Badflower
I Fall Apart – Post Malone
Die Young – MRKTS
Just Breathe – Pearl Jam
Die Like This – Mourners
Unconditional – Matt Maeson
Grace – Lewis Capaldi

ACKNOWLEDGMENTS

The list is long for all those who had a hand in this book, and at the same time, it's impossibly small.

This book was originally published in a different world created by an author I love and admire. The honor of being able to create in her world is hard to put words to. It was big, and scary, and amazing all at the same time. Add to that, the when and where it was written: in the midst of the world being shut down and my city at the time burning down around me. The emotions in this story come with a side of true and honest tears. There is reality within the pages of each of my stories—altered in some cases, but there nonetheless.

Below are the mostly original acknowledgements with the updated information in italics. And, as always, Thank You!

Thank you to my dear sweet husband who has been behind me on this project in a way that I struggle to put into words. After years of military service, it took a civilian job to put us through our longest separation from each other, and I am so happy to be back in the same town with you again! Talking plot, walking the dogs with me when I get stuck. Ordering food and swinging by the liquor store, you've kept me going.

To Jane Ashley Converse for the cover image that captured Miles perfectly and Stacy Garcia for creating the most perfect cover for this story.

To Dee Hays for patting my head, kicking my butt, making me laugh, and sending the best encouragement my way. This couldn't have happened without you.

To Jennifer Rebecca for the plot twist idea that made me gasp and shake in my shoes.

To my dear friends for keeping me in line, for urging me to write when the world was falling down around us, and for making time for me. To talk. To whine. To drink whiskey over zoom.

And finally, to the people of Total Wine. This book was written from the guest bedroom of my new-to-me-but-very-old house, during a full kitchen renovation that came to a standstill due to the pandemic shutdown. It was an adventure.

Thank you, always, to my readers and the members of my FB reader group for bearing with me, and to the new readers who have taken a chance on me here. I appreciate each of you.

MORE BOOKS BY THE AUTHOR

Beekman Hills Series
> *Troubles*
> *Twist*
> *Tombstones*
> *Beekman Hills Box Set*

Stand Alone Title
> *Sweet on You*

UnBroken: the series
> *In Tune*
> *Off Bass*
> *Beat Down*
> *Out Loud* Coming Soon (Follow me on BookBub or Good-Reads for release alerts)

Karin is a New York Girl living in a Midwest world. A connoisseur of great words, fine bourbon, and strong coffee, she's married to the love of her life and is mother to two grown men that she is proud to say can cook and clean up after themselves, and always open doors for the ladies thanks to the Rules of Being a Gentleman (you're welcome, world).
Her one major vice is rescuing and adopting big dogs.
Tons of personality, not so good on manners.
She loves talking books, hearing from readers, and hosting the occasional virtual
Happy Hour in her reading group.

www.kcenderswrites.com

facebook.com/kcewrites
instagram.com/authorkcenders
bookbub.com/profile/kc-enders
goodreads.com/author